Bedding the Billionaire

Book 3

The Legacy Collection

Ruth Cardello

Author Contact
website: RuthCardello.com
email: ruthcardello@gmail.com
Facebook: Author Ruth Cardello
Twitter: RuthieCardello

Lil Dartley's life is upside down. Her previously steadfast and predictable sister is marrying an influential billionaire and needs help planning the wedding of the century in less than a month. Years of middle-class rebellion have not prepared Lil for handling billionaires or paparazzi.

Jake Walton knows a train wreck when he sees one. Lil was trouble from the first day he met her, but since her sister is marrying his best friend, he has no choice but to help her or this wedding will be in the news for all the wrong reasons. Keeping Lil safe would be a whole lot easier if she didn't drive him crazy both in and out of the bedroom.

Copyright

Dedication

To Carmen Sonnes, an artist who kindly allowed me to feature her story and her artwork in this book. Please visit my website for more information about her.

And to my parents, two incredible people, who taught me everything I know about family, friendship and the resiliency of love. I miss them both every day.

Chapter One

(Before you start reading, consder signing up for Ruth Cardello's newsletter. Don't miss a release or sale.)
forms.aweber.com/form/58/1378607658.htm

"LOOKING FOR MORE about the Corisi/Dartley whirlwind romance? We have an exclusive interview with the bride-to-be's sister." The promo from a Boston news station played on the phone Jake Walton had propped on a table in his room-sized closet as he was getting dressed one morning.

Jake paused briefly from looping his carefully chosen, blue silk tie in a full Windsor. Most men were aware of one or two ways to knot a tie, but Jake knew over eighty methods to perform that simple function and how each conveyed a subtle, yet different message. Information was power, even when applied to the details.

The video clip his business partner, Dominic Corisi, had sent his phone a few moments earlier was not welcome information, but since the actual interview had yet to air there was time to squash it. Having a network of security in a variety of cities had paid off again.

This was an unfortunate distraction for Dominic at the very time when he most needed to regain his focus. Luckily the situation could easily be rectified with a few phone calls and would hopefully be quickly forgotten by the public.

No doubt, Dominic's next step would be to call him, perpetuating the cycle they had fallen into years ago—Dominic made a mess and always expected Jake to clean it up. Jake didn't deny that there was a certain pleasure to be found in bringing order to the chaos his business partner often left in his wake. Normally something like this interview would be categorized as a minor nuisance. Dominic was famous for being volatile, impulsive, and often the subject of legal inquires, certainly not a man who feared bad press, but with Corisi Enterprises having invested so much into one contract with China, the stakes were insanely high.

Jake resumed knotting his tie as he watched the rest of the video clip.

"Listen as Lil Dartley spills her true feelings about having billionaire and computer tycoon Dominic Corisi kidnap her sister. Hear her confess something that is sure to rock the Corisi camp. Think you know the whole story? You don't know this. Don't miss our exclusive phone interview—tonight at seven."

Surely Dominic hadn't been careless enough to share the one piece of information that could topple Corisi Enterprises? If so, no amount of money could stifle her interview.

Was Lil making a grab for her five minutes of fame, or something more insidious? She was a young, single mother of twenty-five. It wasn't unimaginable that she'd think the world owed her something since her sister had hit the proverbial jackpot by snagging a billionaire.

Normally the exposure of human flaw did not elicit more than annoyance from Jake, but it was oddly disappointing to find it so soon in Dominic's new family—Lil in particular. Not that her character, or lack of, should matter one way or another to Jake. *She was, and always should have been, off-limits.*

A memory from the first time he'd met her came back to him with disconcerting clarity. His body tightened and warmed as if she were once again standing before him, defiantly flipping her cascade of dark brown curls over one shoulder and waving her other hand back and forth as if underlying her words.

"You lied to me," she'd accused. And waited, practically tapping a foot in displeasure. The details of the bowling alley she'd dragged him to that night had faded away, but the fullness of her pouting mouth remained painfully easy to recall.

"You asked me if I liked to bowl, not if I knew how." A hint of self-satisfaction had spilled into his tone and it'd bothered him. Knocking over a set of pins with a spinning projectile was a simple process of aiming for a "pocket," the space between the front pin and the one angled behind it to the right. Not a difficult feat if you understood angles and velocity. So why had he puffed up with pride over this achievement?

Lil.

His realization that he wanted to impress her had been

the most unsettling part of the evening. There had been far too much going on with Corisi Enterprises to waste time on what the little sister of Dominic's latest fling thought of him. He'd scowled down at her, more in response to his own thoughts than to her words.

Money shaped how most people interacted with him, but it wasn't something that he'd given much reflection to until he'd met Lil. Her displeasure with the reason for his visit had initially outweighed whatever most women found attractive about him. She hadn't asked him to join her that night because she wanted to spend more time with him.

No, she'd taken him outside of what she'd considered his comfort zone with a less than noble goal, but she'd failed. "Disappointed that I don't look ridiculous?" he'd asked.

She'd rested a hand on one jean-clad hip, looking him up and down, smirking as she'd noted the clash between his Dayang suit and his colorful, rented bowling shoes; a perusal that had sent his blood rushing to places he thought he'd gained control of by his late teens. "Oh, you still do, don't worry."

More than the way her yellow T-shirt had clung to her small but tempting endowments, or how her jeans had been tight in all the right places—what had driven his blood pressure higher had been the bold challenge in her eyes. He'd never been the type of man who reached out, grabbed with passion, and took. But that night, he'd wanted to be.

Instead, he'd adjusted his tie and cleared his throat. "Then I suggest you beat my score or risk the same fate."

She'd continued to assess him, shaking her head slightly.

"I don't get you. I mean, aren't you Dominic's second in command?"

The memory of that comment elicited the same tight smile it had the first time he'd heard it. "Something like that."

"Don't you mind *babysitting* me?"

Her question had highlighted the heart of the problem.

He should.

His business partner was having a very public breakdown in the middle of one of the most important business deals in the history of their company. He should have accompanied Dominic to China and ensured that his current altered state of mind didn't leave him open to manipulation.

Instead he'd allowed Dominic to sidetrack him with a trip to Boston.

A trip that should have ended after he'd ascertained Lil's safety from the security detail that Dominic had sent to watch her. However, something had happened when she'd opened the door of her house, baby on one hip, long rebellious tendrils framing her naturally beautiful face. He'd felt the floor sway beneath his usually steady feet.

Her growing irritation with him as he'd explained who he was had taken him by surprise; as had her blatant desire for him to leave. He wasn't accustomed to women dismissing him quite so easily. Feeling a bit like he was peddling something door to door, he'd almost failed to gain entry to her house.

And he'd enjoyed every moment of it.

Her irritation had returned with force at the bowling

alley, but had softened to include a semi-apology. "Sorry, I shouldn't take my bad mood out on you, but I am perfectly capable of surviving a few days without my sister. Wasn't the nanny enough? How much supervision does she think I need?" When he'd opened his mouth to say something, she'd said, "Don't answer that. It was a rhetorical question."

He must not have hidden his amusement well because her eyes had narrowed in the most adorable, piqued expression. "Laugh away but I just lost all sympathy for you. You're going down."

Her comment had found its target. His breath had quickened in response as he'd met her audaciously bold, amber glare. "I never lose."

She'd leaned closer as if testing something.

He'd sucked his breath in surprise.

Placing a hand on one of his shoulders, she'd stretched up on her tiptoes and whispered in his ear, "Neither do I." Her hand trailed halfway down his buttoned shirt as she turned away.

He'd stood immobile, watching the seductive sway of her hips as she sauntered over to retrieve her ball. Just before she'd released it, she'd looked over her shoulder at him, catching the guilty shift of his attention from her amazing ass to the sass in those brown eyes. Her wink had almost been his undoing.

His body had surged and craved.

Strike.

Triumphantly, she'd brushed by him, touching him only with her fresh scent. Normally he would have said that he had little preference regarding female perfumes, but that evening he'd discovered the lack of one to be strikingly attractive, sending his thoughts in wild directions—some that had included how the waxed lane would feel beneath their bare skin.

With what could only have been described as a saucy smile, she'd said, "Your turn."

He'd chosen his next ball at random.

Thrown it without thought.

Barely registered that it had left most of the pins standing.

Just as his second had.

Her chuckle had removed his last shred of restraint.

Closing the distance between them, he'd placed a hand on either side of her face and tasted her smiling lips. Just a brief touch, a flick of a tongue, nothing that should have overshadowed his usual distaste for public displays of affection. Such banal behavior was never necessary, but to his surprise he'd found it, oh, so pleasurable.

Her humor had melted beneath the heat of their connection and her tongue had begun a teasing dance of its own. He'd stopped hearing the blaring background music, stopped listening to the inner voice that warned him that he was losing control. He'd kissed her until her arms had curled around his neck, until her back had arched to press her closer to him, and until her breathing had become as hot and ragged as his.

Eventually the hoots of encouragement and echoing catcalls from players in other lanes had registered and Jake had ended the kiss. Heart pounding in his chest, he'd mentally scrambled to regain his decorum, but his body had continued to betray him by not releasing her.

Achieving his level of power and success so quickly meant that he spent most of his time in boardrooms with people almost twice his age. Around Lil, he'd felt impulsive and younger. Leaning in for one final taste of her lips, he'd whispered against them, "Your turn," and had chuckled at how quickly her bemusement had been replaced by ire.

She'd spun away, picked up her ball, and presented him with her tempting ass and an over-the-shoulder smirk before strutting to the lane.

Game on.

BACK IN HIS New York townhouse, Jake adjusted his already straight tie, and donned a charcoal, Brioni pinstriped jacket. Not many would get his subtle clothing humor, but recently he'd purchased a few of the suits that were famous for their James Bond affiliation. As he smoothed the perfectly tailored shoulders, he dismissed Lil as the reason he'd decided to walk on the wilder side of business attire.

After all, nothing had actually happened that night.

A call from the security detail he'd sent to China with Dominic had swiftly ended whatever had been building between Lil and him. Someone had been meeting with the Chinese minister of commerce while Dominic had returned to the States for the reading of his father's will, news that threatened a contract they'd considered a done deal. Jake had flown to Beijing immediately after unceremoniously depositing Lil on her doorstep.

Ideally, that would have been the last he'd seen of Lil.

Then her call had come, begging him to help her find her sister. He'd flown her to Isola Santos. The sexual tension had been fast and furious between them, especially when they'd met up in the kitchen that first night, but he had wisely turned down her flirtatious offer to explore what was between them. With his business partner and his finances potentially out of control, his personal life needed to remain in order.

Sex could wait until after the present crisis had been resolved.

Not that his love-sick business partner would agree.

Dominic's obsession with Abby Dartley could not have come at a worse time; he was going to lose everything if he didn't wake up soon. Jake had invested too much time into their company to idly sit back and watch Dominic piss it away.

Jake's cell phone rang. *Speak of the devil.*

"Jake, I need you up in Boston," Dominic said with an abruptness that was somewhat comforting.

"Dominic, I was just thinking about you." And Boston.

"Did you see the video I sent you?" Dominic asked with complete disregard to niceties and continued on without waiting for Jake's response. "Abby called her sister, but she's not picking up her phone. Fly up there and see what's going on."

"No," Jake said and surprised himself with his conviction on the matter. "This is an easy fix. I'll have Duhamel make a few calls."

Slowly, with comical emphasis, Dominic said, "You just said *no*. You never say no."

"That's because you don't normally ask me to do something that is a complete waste of my time. I've got a couple leads on programmers. I intend to meet with one this afternoon." Programmers who could hopefully do what none of the ones he'd spoken to thus far had proven successful at—remove the virus Stephan Andrade's hacker had uploaded to their server.

"I need you up in Boston more."

Jake took a deep breath. "Dominic, do you understand that you could lose everything if we don't do something fast?"

Dominic countered, "I am working on it."

Balancing his phone on one shoulder, he tied one of his dress shoes impatiently and scoffed, "I'd like nothing more than to believe that."

"When have I ever lost a deal?"

"Burundi, Guinea, Andorra, Chile . . ." The list was endless.

"We closed on every one of those."

"By the skin of our teeth." *And because I have become adept at justifying your outrageous antics.*

"Suddenly you're afraid of a challenge?"

"This is different, Dom. You've got too much riding on this one deal. Don't tie me up with nonsense when the clock is ticking against us."

For just a moment, Jake thought Dominic was about to

concede that Jake was right.

Dominic said, "I've opened a dialogue with two people who have the skills we need and they will be at my house this weekend. If it makes you feel better, I'll let you finalize the details."

Jake stopped, suddenly alert. "Who? Who did you find?"

Dominic hedged. "We shouldn't talk about this on the phone."

Finally, something that made sense. "Right. Where do you want to meet?"

"I need you in Boston for this Lil thing first."

An uncomfortable vision of Lil's taunting smile surfaced, distracting Jake for a moment before he forced himself to refocus on the issue at hand. His irritation with himself was evident in his tone when he said, "Why don't you go?"

"Abby made me promise not to get involved. She wants Lil to work this out on her own."

"And sending me doesn't count?"

A serious tone filled Dominic's voice. "She's not safe, Jake. Lil is not prepared for all the media attention she is getting or how that has made her a potential target. She thinks she can handle it, but you know that she and her baby are vulnerable to everything from manipulation to outright kidnapping. I can't believe you're not already on this. This interview is just the tip of an iceberg of potential problems."

It was never a good sign when Jake had to concede that Dominic had a point.

Jake didn't want to think about Lil being vulnerable. He didn't want to think about her at all, but now that Dominic had brought up the possibility of Lil being in danger he had to acknowledge the reality of the threat.

"Have you explained this to Abby?"

Dominic groaned. "I tried. Dartley women are stubborn. I sent a nanny, Lil sent her back. I had security watching her house twenty-four seven, Lil threatened to call the police if they stayed. I even bought that girl a damned penthouse in downtown Boston, in a very secure building, but she won't budge. She said she doesn't want or need my money. She won't even use the driver I sent."

Oh, Dominic.

"That's a lot of involvement for a man who promised to stay out of it."

"That's what Abby said."

"The only thing you didn't do was drag her down to New York against her will." Jake pocketed his wallet. How a man like Dominic stayed out of jail was often a mystery to Jake, but it was that unpredictable element about him that made him so successful in business.

"Trust me, I thought about it."

"Dominic—"

"Don't worry, I'm not going to do anything rash. That's why I'm sending you. Consider this a . . ."

"Don't say it, Dom. Don't even go there. I've spent the last week flying all over the country trying to save your ass. Your favor account has been depleted."

"I'm not sure I like the new you, Jake," Dominic growled.

Jake headed down the stairs to get his morning cup of

black coffee. "I'm not the one who changed, Dom. You need to get your head back in the game before you lose everything."

And I need to stay focused.

Which meant going to see Lil was out of the question.

Not a man who could be accused of playing fair, Dominic added, "Don't force me to bring out the big guns over this."

"You wouldn't," Jake said with annoyance, and put his coffee mug down, untouched.

"I will if you leave me no other choice."

That was also how Dominic won—with a long history of following through with his threats. It was never a case of if he would do it, but rather a question of whether or not you could handle a particular consequence of denying him.

Often, it was simply easier to work around him instead of against him.

Once Lil was safely deposited in her new, highly secure abode and the interview was a non-issue, Jake would try to reason with Dominic again. "Fine, and I'll handle the interview while I'm there. Duhamel can arrange the details of the move. I'll get Lil in the penthouse by tonight but after that, I'm not promising anything. I can't make her stay there."

"You can talk anyone into anything."

Not true. I've been trying to talk you back from crazy for over a month.

Dominic added, "Oh, one more thing. See that she comes down to New York on Friday. This is an important

13

weekend for us."

Seriously?

Jake leaned against the kitchen counter. "Dom, are they worth this? This family that you're so attached to? Do you really think they're going to stick around if you're a mail clerk next year?"

"Yes," he said in a tone that took Jake aback. "Yes, I do."

"I sure hope you're right, Dom, because I don't know if we're going to make our deadline."

"I've got a plan, Jake. Don't worry."

It wasn't the first time he'd heard that claim.

He hoped it was true this time. "I'll be back by Wednesday and then we'll talk about who you've lined up. I should prep before I meet with them," Jake said.

Dominic said, "Don't worry, you know them."

"I do?" Jake didn't think he'd left one computer-savvy acquaintance off his list.

Dominic said, "I'm counting on it. Call me if you hit a snag in Boston."

And you'll do what? "I won't."

"Oh, and try to make it sound like it was your idea to go."

That request did not even warrant a reply.

Jake shook his head at the phone and hung up.

How the mighty Dominic had fallen.

Jake packed an overnight bag and made arrangements for his luxury helicopter. He'd chosen this particular New York building as his home because the generous roof had allowed him to install a private landing pad. Sure, a jet would have gotten him to Boston faster, but he liked the increased landing opportunities that helicopters offered. His could fly six people with the same quiet comfort of a limo directly to one of his buildings without the hassle of dealing with traffic. A helicopter with that level of sound insulation and refinement cost more than many private jets, but it was one of the few luxuries Jake found pleasure in owning.

Once in the city, he usually rented a private car and drove himself. He preferred less pomp and circumstance and found the constant presence of someone, especially those attempting to anticipate his every need, extremely tiring.

For that reason, his house staff came on Mondays and Thursdays while he was at work. They cleaned his home, stocked his shelves, and left a few pre-made meals that he could microwave if he didn't wish to order out. The only evidence of the staff's existence was the constant availability of everything he required.

Nice and neat.

Just the way he liked his life.

LIL PEERED OUT the window by pulling down one blind just enough to see through it and groaned. A flock of press had descended on her small house in the suburbs of Boston almost immediately after the promo of her tell-all interview had televised. They had been there all day.

She glanced down at the baby who was still happily play-ing on her back in the middle of a small blanket, kicking at the toys that hung from an arch above her. "Colby, what am I going to do?"

The only way the news station could have an interview from her was if the woman who had called yesterday claiming to be her sister's new personal assistant had lied. That possibility was unacceptable because it would mean that her entire practice session on how to field questions from the press had been recorded. It would also mean that a host of things she would never have shared, if not for the jovial tone of the fake interview, were about to be made public.

She didn't need this today.

Having already completed the final assignments for two of her three remaining college courses, this week was supposed to revolve around studying for tomorrow's final exam in integrated office systems. One more class and she'd have an Administrative Assistant degree. Not her ideal job, but one that would bring in a stable income.

If I don't fail my final course. Or, make myself unemployable with stunts like this. She'd gotten several calls regarding her resume since she'd blanketed the local area with it. Would this TV fiasco ruin her chances? It certainly wasn't going to improve them.

Her cell phone showed three missed calls from Abby.

Colby rolled into a seated position and gurgled up at her mother.

"You're right, Colby. Mommy's just too proud to ask her for help. Auntie Abby would fix this, just like she's always fixed everything and the worst part is that she wouldn't even be angry with me. She expects me to do shit like this. Hell, why shouldn't she? This is what I do."

Sucking on one fist, Lil's daughter met her eyes with the concern of a child who only knows that her mother isn't happy but doesn't know why.

Lil continued on as if her daughter could understand. "How could I have done this?"

From the moment she'd received the news that she was carrying a new life within her, something in her had shifted. One incredibly painful weekend of self-reflection had birthed some difficult resolutions. No more letting Abby support her, clean up after her, save her from the consequences of her actions. No more lamenting on what she thought her life should have been.

It was time to grow up.

Although she'd always stood up for her beliefs and done what she'd thought was the right thing, where had it gotten her?

A long string of dead-end jobs.

A future that was as bleak as her bank account.

Not a life you bring a baby into.

So, Lil had enrolled in college courses and resolved to stop compulsively speaking her mind—at least where her employers were concerned. Too bad she hadn't kept her thoughts to herself when Abby had asked her opinion of Dominic. Of course, there was no way she could have known how wildly in love her sister would fall or how much of an effect that relationship would have on her own life.

Dominic seemed to have good intentions and it wasn't that his offers of financial assistance weren't tempting, but any proximity to him was a bit like inviting a tornado into your yard—he didn't understand boundaries and without meaning to he could destroy everything you've worked for.

If Abby was overprotective, Dominic was downright smothering.

At first, he hadn't accepted her declaration that what she really wanted from the both of them was the freedom to stand on her own two feet. After a few verbal scuffles, things had calmed and Lil had started to feel that Abby and Dominic finally understood.

I just want time to prove to myself that I'm not a complete screwup.

And I was doing fine . . . until this morning.

Lil groaned.

Mothers don't embarrass themselves in the news.

Mothers were supposed to be steadfast and responsible.

At least, that was the type of mother Lil remembered having when she was younger and it was the kind of mother Abby had become to her when their parents had died in a car crash when Lil was thirteen.

Abby would never have spoken to that woman without double-checking her credentials. She wouldn't have let her bruised ego get the better of her and spouted those comments about Jake. She definitely wouldn't be hiding in her house hoping this would all magically go away.

Outside of Dominic, Abby was as impulsive as the sunset.

And I'm about as reliable as the weatherman.

Poor Colby, you chose the wrong womb.

Instead of cheering her, the joke brought unexpected

tears of frustration to Lil's eyes. *It doesn't have to be like that anymore. A person can change if they want to badly enough.* "I'm going to be a good mother to you, Colby. I promise you that. I'm going to be someone you can be proud of." It was hard to feel bad for herself when her daughter held up two drool covered hands in a silent request to be picked up. Lil cuddled her baby into her neck and shook her head sadly. "Right after this one last screwup."

In her moment of need, she reached for the impossible.

I wish you were here, Mom. I don't know if I can do this without you. What if I can't be the person I'm trying to be? What if Colby pays the price because I can't get my shit together?

There was no chill to the room, no apparition or voice from beyond, but for just a moment Lil felt her mother with her and a tear escaped down her cheek. Her young daughter patted it away with a coo.

You're right, Mom. It's going to be okay because I will make it okay. I'm a strong, independent woman and I don't need anyone to solve my problems for me.

The news station had tricked her into giving an interview. That had to be illegal. She needed a lawyer. One of her high school friends had just passed the bar. Maybe he could write up something that would force the station to pull the tape.

With Colby on one hip, Lil dialed the number of a woman she loved like family. "Mrs. Lawson, is Aaron home?"

"Lil! I was going to call you, but I figured your phone must be ringing off the wall. Are you okay? I saw the news."

An explanation gushed out of her. "I didn't give the interview. Well, I did, but I didn't mean to. Some woman called and pretended to be Abby's assistant and I fell for it. She told me that Abby had asked her to prep me for potential questions from the press."

"Oh, honey. I figured it was something like that. You must be a wreck. What did Abby say?"

"I haven't actually spoken to her about it yet." Lil had been trying, somewhat unsuccessfully, to avoid Abby since the night on the island when she'd made a complete fool out of herself by confusing Jake's light flirtation with something more serious. If she never saw him again, it would be too soon. She didn't want to tell Abby about that humiliating night any more than she wanted to explain her latest folly.

Mrs. Lawson clucked her disapproval, but only said, "Well, Aaron is home, but he's sleeping. What do you need?"

Lil chewed her bottom lip before asking, "Do you think he could write up something that threatens the station with legal action if they go forward with airing it? I'm hoping if I get it there this morning they will pull the interview."

"Of course he can! I'll go wake him up. This will be good for him. He's been applying for jobs since he graduated, but you know him—he won't accept a position that requires he relocates. I love that boy, but he worries about me too much. It's not healthy. He's starting to get depressed. If he doesn't find something soon, he's going to have to start up his lawn business again or he won't be able to pay his college loans. Maybe someone will notice him through this and offer him something local."

"I hope so! Thanks. Tell him I'll be there in about thirty minutes. I'm just going to change and pack Colby up." Lil began to mentally review the outfits in her closet. Luckily she'd purchased a navy jacket and skirt for her interviews. Wasn't navy the choice of those who wanted to be taken seriously?

I hope it's the color that says, "I mean it, I'll sue you."

Mrs. Lawson said, "I'm sorry you're going through this, Lil, but it'll be nice to see you. What if I make you lunch? Just like the old days?"

"I won't be able to stay. I've got to get to the station early if I'm going to stop this from happening."

"I'll brown bag it for you."

"You don't have to go to any trouble."

Mrs. Lawson was insistent. "No trouble, Lil. Aaron wouldn't have made it out of high school without you. If you won't marry him and make me happy, the least you can do is let me feed you."

"You know we don't feel like that about each other."

The older woman sighed. "I know, but a mother can dream."

No, they can't, Lil wanted to say. *Mothers have to put their dreams aside and start making responsible decisions.*

Mrs. Lawson knew Lil well enough to sense her real distress. She made a sympathetic sound and said, "It'll work out, Lil. You just get yourself together and come on over early. You've got a big day head of you."

Lil agreed, hung up and carried Colby to the bedroom with her. She tied her hair up in what she hoped was a serious looking bun. Her confidence increased as she layered on the armor of her business attire.

A stranger stared back at her in the mirror. What did people say? "Dress for the job you want, not the job you have." In this case, she was dressing for the person she wanted to be. If the shoes were too tight and the skirt felt restrictive, well it was something she was determined to learn to love.

She gathered Colby's supplies.

Bottles. Check. Diapers and wipes. Check. Puff snacks. Check.

A big day.

She slung a diaper bag over her shoulder and secured Colby into her portable car seat.

That's one way to describe it. All I have to do is get by the reporters, get the letter and convince a station manager that pulling an interview and receiving flack for doing it will be preferable to whatever litigation Aaron chooses to threaten them with.

Completely doable.

As long as the day doesn't hold any more surprises.

Chapter Two

M AKING IT TO the car wasn't as bad as Lil had anticipated. With a hand shielding Colby from the flashes of
cameras, Lil had rushed through the press, refusing to
respond to the questions they'd thrown at her.

"How much did they pay you for the interview, Lil?"

"What's your big confession?"

"Are you doing this because you're jealous of your sister's
recent publicity?"

After securing Colby in the back seat, Lil hastily slid into
the driver's seat of her little, red Ford Focus and breathed
with relief. Unfortunately, she wasn't going to get anywhere
very fast with those reporters blocking her driveway. She
considered simply backing up and forcing them to scramble.
That's what the old her would have done in a heartbeat and
she wouldn't have given a thought to possible consequences.

The new her was trying to figure out how not to give
them another reason to feature her on the news tonight.

Her cell phone rang.

Jake.

Great. That's the last person I want to talk to right now.

When she didn't answer, he merely rang again.

Impatiently swiping her phone to connect, she said, "What do you want, Jake? I'm a little busy right now." She'd given up trying to impress him.

"Where are you going?"

The hair on the back of her neck rose. "How do you know I'm going anywhere?"

"I'm parked across the street."

A quick turn confirmed his claim.

"Shit." Lil quickly checked her daughter in the mirror. "Don't worry, Colby, Mommy is going to stop swearing after today. Don't remember any of this."

"Are you talking to me?" Jake asked.

"No," Lil shook her head. "Sorry. I was——." Lil stopped herself from sharing what would only make her sound crazier than she already felt. "What are you doing here, Jake?"

"I wanted to see you."

If only that were true.

"You mean Dominic sent you."

"Does it matter?"

It shouldn't, but it did. There could never be anything between them; he'd said so himself. Those words still stung even all these weeks later.

"Not at all."

"Why did you give the interview, Lil?"

"I didn't——" Once again, she stopped herself. She didn't owe him an explanation. "You can tell Dominic that I have the situation under control. The interview won't be airing."

"Did you have a change of heart?"

"Think what you want, Jake, but think it in New York. I'm having a bad enough day."

Jake hung up.

Lil watched him exit his silver BMW, every bit as immaculately groomed as the last time she'd seen him. He towered a good foot above the reporters, but Lil was sure that wasn't what made them take a step back as he approached them. Jake wore wealth and influence like some people wore an old coat, with comfortable indifference. He didn't doubt for a moment that people should respect him and wasn't surprised when they did.

Whatever he said to the reporters was tempered with a smooth smile. The combination worked, they responded by reorganizing their cameras on the opposite side of the road with seemingly no complaint.

No one should be that good-looking and that powerful.

Life should bestow one.

Getting both was just plain unfair.

She fought the impulse to drive off while he was otherwise occupied.

He strode toward her car and she caught her breath. *No wonder I threw myself at him. I mean, look at him.*

Damn.

She'd almost convinced herself that she'd exaggerated his attractiveness in her memories. No, it was all there—the classically square jaw, perfectly styled dark brown hair, expertly tailored clothing that accentuated his muscular frame and golden-brown eyes that sent shivers of excitement down her spine as they seared through the distance between them.

Could any woman be blamed for wanting to believe that lightning could strike twice in one family? Her sister had gotten her own fairy-tale ending, why couldn't the universe have sent Lil one?

In retrospect, the possibility lacked precedent.

Even the Grimms knew—one Prince Charming per village.

That made Jake the wolf?

More like a crappy narrator who breaks in to remind you that none of it is real.

He yanked the door open and slid into the passenger seat. The subtle scent of his cologne teased and tempted.

Okay, an incredibly sexy, crappy narrator.

She gripped the steering wheel and focused on the dash-board.

Gorgeous men who don't want to be with you shouldn't be so difficult to avoid.

To fill the silence she said, "Thank you for whatever you just said to the press. Now I really have to go. I'm already late."

"For?" The click of his seat belt being secured echoed in the small car.

"If you must know, I'm seeing my lawyer this morning. He's writing up a gag order for the interview which I will then deliver to the station manager and this whole thing will hopefully just go away."

"So, you didn't sell the story."

"No, I didn't."

"I'll come with you."

Of course you will, Lil thought, but said, "I don't suppose you'll believe me if I tell you that I can handle it myself?"

Those beautiful eyes stared blandly back at her.

Lil turned away from him again.

"Lil," he commanded softly with just the use of her name. Lil reluctantly met his eyes again. "You have no reason to be embarrassed around me. I wanted to take you up on your offer that night, but it would have complicated an already difficult situation."

What the hell did that even mean?

"I didn't *offer* you anything," she denied hotly.

"Then you have even less of a reason to feel awkward around me."

"I don't—" Heat rushed up her neck. What was the use of denying what was blatantly true? "Can we leave that night in the past? This is about today. I don't need your help. And I'd like you to get out of my car."

"You know I'm not leaving until this situation is resolved."

Her heart flipped in her chest. There was nothing about the situation that needed to be resolved. She'd let the emotions of the weekend overtake her common sense. A man like Jake could have his pick of women; he didn't need the complication of a young mother. And he'd said as much, rather clearly, when he'd explained that he didn't see how there could ever be anything between them.

As her embarrassment ran its course, a more painful realization came to her.

He wasn't referring to *that* situation.

This was about the interview—nothing more.

She lashed out at him. "Because you do everything Dominic tells you to do?"

The bastard didn't even flinch, just inclined his head slightly and said, "When it suits me. And right now I need to know exactly what you said in that interview."

No, you don't.

Lil ground the engine when she started the car for the second time. "It doesn't matter what I said because the interview is never going to air."

"Finally, something we agree on."

His unflappable calm sent a wave of angry adrenaline coursing through Lil. She backed out of her driveway with too much force and heard the crunch of her garbage can beneath her rear tires. She had to pull forward, back up, and pull forward again to dislodge it from beneath the vehicle.

She looked at him quickly, daring him to say a word.

Quite wisely, he didn't.

ANOTHER MAN WOULD have needed to drive, but that wasn't how Jake operated. Very rarely was the figurehead of any situation the one who was actually in control. By charging forward, most people limited their potential. Few took time to analyze and take advantage of the spectrum of possible outcomes to any given decision.

Like choosing to drive.

Had he demanded the wheel, he wouldn't have been able to study Lil's profile.

He would have missed the curve of her breast that the seat belt revealed as it pulled back one side of her jacket and pushed the material of her blouse aside in the most tantalizing way. She really was stunning.

Too bad she was completely unsuitable for him. He preferred a woman with a certain level of sophistication; one who understood that relationships worked best if emotional extremes were avoided. Pleasant, predictable conversation with someone who seamlessly blended with diplomats and was also good in bed was enough to keep him satisfied.

So why was he ogling her chest while imagining what it would be like to slip a hand beneath the hem of her skirt and beg her to pull the car over on a side road so he could touch her, taste her, fill her?

Because his mind and his body were definitely at odds regarding Lil.

Colby made a sound in the back seat, reminding him of the reality of the situation. Leering felt wrong with a child present and represented another reason his attraction to Lil made no sense.

He didn't get involved with women who had children.

Not that he and Lil were involved.

Damn.

I should have followed my instincts and stayed the hell in New York.

He shifted uncomfortably and turned to look out the passenger window.

Get a grip, Jake.

If all went according to his plan, and things usually did,

tonight would see Lil tucked away in her new penthouse in Boston, the interview nothing more than a quickly forgotten blip, and him back in New York.

There was no way he was going to stick around to bring Lil to New York for the weekend. Dominic could come and get her himself if he wanted her there so badly.

"Your shirt is open," he said gruffly without looking away from the lane of traffic outside the window.

"Oh, my God, it is," Lil said, swerving the car a bit as she adjusted it.

He caught himself smiling in the reflection of the window, and then frowned. Just because she amused him, didn't change the facts.

He was not there to indulge himself. This was business.

Well, business related.

"Sorry—" she started to say and then stopped abruptly. When she continued, her tone implied that she'd had a thought that quite amused her. "Was it bothering you?"

He whipped around to look at her. "No," he said. "No," he said again. And then because he had a mastery of the spoken language that had impressed many a politician, he added, "No," one last time.

She tried, but failed, to contain her amusement.

"It's okay if it was," she said impishly and patted his leg in a pretense of support, outright mocking him, right down to the tone he'd used earlier. "You have no reason to be embarrassed around me."

His body leapt in response to her challenge even as his mind fought for control. He growled, "You simply shouldn't walk around with your shirt hanging open."

"So it was a public service announcement?"

"Yes, unless that's how you planned to compensate your lawyer."

Her hand flew off his lap and she muttered something that sounded suspiciously like "Jackass" under her breath.

Jake turned to look out the window again, hopefully before his face had revealed how much he wanted to kiss that profanity off her sweet lips.

Chapter Three

"I THOUGHT WE were going to see your lawyer," Jake said as Lil parked her car in front of the Lawson's home in a typical, working-class neighborhood with manicured lawns and children riding their bikes on the sidewalks.

"We are," she answered simply, opening the car door instead of providing further explanation. Her friend might not have a fancy city office, but he was brilliant and Lil trusted him.

"He lives here?" Jake asked, perhaps noting the swing that hung from the porch and the flower pots that lined the stairs.

"Yes," Lil said in a clipped tone, slamming the car door behind her after freeing Colby from her car seat and collecting her diaper bag. She turned and faced him. "If you have any smart remarks to share, say them here. These people are like family to me."

He looked instantly taken aback. "I would never."

He probably wouldn't.

A man like him would have impeccable manners.

He didn't have to try to make most people feel inferior;

it was a natural byproduct of being near someone who had been born with too much of . . . well, everything.

"Just try to look a little less—pompous."

One eyebrow rose.

Before moving forward, Lil added, "Aaron isn't like you. He's . . ." She hesitated.

"Don't stop there; I'm dying to know what he is that I'm not."

"Sensitive." Aaron would cringe if he heard her describe him that way, and perhaps the years had toughened his exterior, but to her he would always be the sixth-grade boy whose pride had often been crushed when he'd been the last child chosen for a recess kickball team.

Just as he'd never let her live down how she'd once socked a boy in the nose for teasing him about not being athletic. Or how, despite Aaron trying to soften her position, she'd remained unrepentant even when brought before the principal. Lil had always believed that bullies should get what they deserved—thus perpetuating what Abby called her inability to respect authority figures.

She did respect them; she just didn't feel that they were infallible.

Sometimes requesting assistance from those in charge simply moved the abuse to somewhere more private. Some things were better addressed head-on and handled yourself. That philosophy had gotten her suspended from school more than once and cost her several jobs.

It had also been why she'd been dubbed the "geek squad's mascot" in the public high school she'd attended.

She never understood why academic excellence had equated to social suicide in the very place where education should have been valued the most. Young men and women who would likely one day run their own companies had hidden in bathrooms instead of risking public degradation at the hands of those who worshipped good looks and huge biceps.

That's how it had been until Lil's freshman year when she'd gone nose to nose with a beefed-up hockey player over something he'd said about the math team winning a regional competition. Lil might not have intervened had the offender not accentuated his comment with a wet napkin assault to the other boy's head as he passed his table.

When Lil suggested that he stop, he'd asked her why she cared and if she were sleeping with one of those man-girls.

And she'd slapped him clean across the face.

He'd leaned down and growled, "You're lucky you're a girl."

She'd growled right back, "So are you."

If only her moment of valor hadn't been witnessed by two supervising teachers who'd cared only that she'd "laid her hands" on another student. The full story had also failed to impress either the principal or Abby.

It had, however, inspired "the geek squad."

If Lil could survive an altercation with the ruling Neanderthal, they could at least claim one table as their own in the cafeteria and hold that ground. And they had.

Abby remembered those years as Lil's most difficult times.

Lil considered them a victorious battleground on which

many lifelong friendships had been forged. With age, she'd learned to use her wit rather than her hands, but she'd never quite mastered keeping her opinion to herself, an affliction that she now saw came at a cost. She hadn't been accepted to any of the art schools she'd applied to. Apparently, her noble intentions didn't excuse repeated suspensions. She could have gone to a community college, but she'd been too proud.

Pride also came with a cost. It had left her in a frustrating limbo—neither working toward her dreams nor choosing new ones. A situation she'd accepted when it had been only her, but Colby deserved better. Luckily the administrative school she was now close to graduating from had decided to give her a chance to prove that she had changed.

"I have no intention of offending your friend." Jake's words jolted Lil back to the present. In truth, Jake had neither said nor done anything that suggested that he would.

Old protective habits die hard.

"Good, because he's extremely intelligent and will make a fantastic lawyer when he finally gets a chance. His mom thinks this will help him."

"He lives with his—"

Lil bristled and spat, "See, he doesn't need that. Not everyone was born into money like you were. He had to work to pay his way through college. He has helped his mother pay the mortgage since his father passed away a few years ago. He's been offered jobs that he hasn't accepted because he doesn't think she'll be able to keep this house up on her own. He has nothing to be ashamed of."

Jake inclined his head in concession to her point.

RUTH CARDELLO

The door swung open and Mrs. Lawson came out onto the porch. She removed the apron from around her waist and laid it across the railing of the porch before reaching out to hug Lil. "Lil!" She swept Colby out of Lil's arms even as she asked, "May I?"

Lil smiled. "That's why I took her out of her seat. I knew you'd want to hold her." Thankfully, some things hadn't changed. Mrs. Lawson still dressed like a TV sitcom mother from the fifties. Her gray hair was perfectly styled in a loose bun and her makeup had been carefully applied even though she likely had nowhere to go that day.

She held Colby up to her face, made her laugh by making a few silly noises and announced, "She's beautiful, Lil. I can't believe how big she has gotten." Then, not relinquishing the baby yet, she turned to Jake and offered her hand in greeting. Jake shook her hand and she said, "Hello, handsome, my name is Ester." Then she smiled at Lil. "So, this is the reason you won't marry my son? Can't say I blame you."

"Mrs. Lawson!"

"What?" She winked at Jake and said. "I'm sixty-seven, not dead."

Jake charmed her with a smile he'd never shown Lil. "I would have guessed forty."

"If I were forty, Lil would be a fool to introduce us. Men like you don't come around every day."

Lil groaned.

The last thing Jake's ego needed was encouragement.

Mrs. Lawson said, "Oh, I'm just teasing. You should see your face, Lil. When did you get so serious? Come on in!

36

Aaron is printing the document for you upstairs in his room. Go on up, I'll show Colby our fish tank."

Lil led the way, each step bringing back another memory from practically growing up in this house. Mrs. Lawson credited Lil with helping Aaron through high school, but the truth was that the same could be said in reverse. This home had been her safe haven when fights had escalated between Abby and her.

It wasn't that Abby had ever done anything unforgivably wrong. Worse, it was how she'd always done everything perfectly right that had set sister against sister. No one could live up to her expectations. At least, Lil couldn't. And when Lil had grown tired of trying to be right, she'd found temporary enjoyment in being blatantly wrong. Most of it had been for show, never more than an attitude or a friendship Abby didn't approve of.

Until Asshole.

He'd been a mistake Abby had warned her about from the first time she'd met him, but Lil hadn't listened. She'd thought she was in love, but she saw now how little she'd really known about that condition.

Dirk had been all sex and no substance. He'd wanted her and to get her he'd been willing to say the four-letter word that she'd longed to hear. He'd said it often and lavishly. He'd said it as much as it took to keep her coming back to him.

He just hadn't said it the night she'd told him that she was pregnant.

No, that night he hadn't said much of anything. Which

was why pride and anger had spurred her to offer him an out; one that he'd taken and never looked back.

Jake was probably doing her a huge favor by not being attracted to her. The last thing she needed was a man right now. She needed to finish school, get a job, and focus on being a good mom.

Jake wasn't a villain. In fact, when she'd needed him to get her to Abby's side, he had helped her without question. Really, the only thing she held against him was that he inspired her to want to rip off her clothes and pounce on a man who could not have been clearer in his rejection of her.

He'd even asked her to reveal less cleavage.

Who does that?

Not a man who is lusting after you, that's who.

Lil knocked on Aaron's bedroom door.

I'M NOT POMPOUS, Jake thought as he waited outside a bedroom door boasting a sign that read, "The force is strong with this one."

A young man, slightly taller than Lil and dressed in gray sweatpants and a college T-shirt opened the door. His dirty-blond hair stuck out wildly in a few places implying that Lil's visit didn't warrant a trip to the mirror.

Jake looked down at his black, conservative Testoni dress shoes and felt a bit overdressed. However, he'd intended to spend the day intimidating a local station manager, not rubbing elbows with someone so fresh from college he probably still hadn't unpacked his diploma.

I only feel about a million years old.

The young man greeted Lil with a smile which fell from his face when he looked past her and saw Jake. "You—you brought Mr. Walton, Lil?"

"You can call me Jake," he said and held out his hand in greeting.

See, not pompous.

Aaron shook his hand profusely, then stepped back and looked like he was questioning the wisdom of inviting them into his room. "It is a real honor to meet you, Mr. Walton. I did a research paper on negotiating techniques that also address consumer perceived ethicality issues. Your success in Moldova was my inspiration." He breathed into a cupped hand as if smelling his breath and made a face. "I don't normally spend my day in my pajamas, but I was . . . I was . . ."

Evidently, lying did not come naturally to this kid. He remembered a time when he'd been the same way. "Lil said you wrote a gag order for the news station."

"I did," Aaron said and awkwardly waved them into his room. "I just printed it out." He stepped over several pieces of laundry on his way to the printer. "Don't mind the mess. I would have cleaned up if I had known you were coming. I thought it was just Lil."

"Perfectly understandable," Jake said and glanced back at Lil.

She was watching the exchange closely.

He wanted to say, "See, you worried about nothing."

The stiff set of her shoulders and that beautifully jutted chin told him that she was prepared to intervene if he stepped out of line with her precious little friend. Since their relationship was clearly not based on anything sexual, he was at a loss for how to categorize it. She'd said he was like family to her. In his experience, *friendships* between men and women were a cover for something less pure. What did she get out of this association? He had a feeling that the answer to that would go a long way toward deepening his understanding of what Lil wanted. And discovering what she wanted only mattered as far as it would help him convince her to accept Dominic's protection. The sooner he did that, the sooner he could return to New York and find out who Dominic thought had the answers they needed.

Jake turned in time to receive a paper from the shaky hands of Lil's "lawyer." His quick skim of the document slowed as he perceived quality. The kid was good. It was well-crafted and as professional as he would have expected from his seasoned lawyers. He nodded. "This is impressive. Good work."

Aaron's face transformed with an ear-to-ear grin. "Thank you. I based it on the Sterling vs. Laudin Communications case."

Lil looked across the room and pinned Jake with those amber eyes of hers. "Good enough that you would write him a letter of reference?"

Aaron's face reddened. "Lil, Mr. Walton doesn't have to do that. He doesn't know me."

It was clear that Lil wanted Aaron to succeed. Why, he couldn't say yet, but it would cost him nothing to toss the boy an opportunity. "I'm always looking for entry level people and we have a branch in Boston. If you send me your resume, I'll give it to my legal department. Then it's up to you to impress them."

"Oh, my God!" He turned to Lil and his grin grew even wider, if that were possible. "Oh, my God!" A spontaneous hug threatened to erupt from him.

Jake held out his hand to deter him.

Aaron shook his hand with enthusiasm. He turned to Lil. "Thank you, Lil! Thank you!" and hugged her.

Jake wanted to rip the little, tail wagging puppy off of Lil, but he didn't. Lil hugged him much longer than he would have liked, but eventually, thankfully stepped back and said, "I didn't do anything, Aaron. You did."

Jake looked down at his watch and pocketed the paper. "We have to go now if we plan to get to the station early."

Lil's eyebrows furrowed, she seemed to want to say something regarding the paper, but instead she said, "I'll get Colby."

She stepped out of the room and Jake had every intention of following her when Aaron stopped him with a hand on his sleeve. "Mr. Walton?"

Jake looked down at the hand, which he expected the boy to hastily remove, but he didn't. Instead Aaron met his eyes with surprising directness.

He said, "A lot of people judge Lil before they know her. She says what she thinks and sometimes she's more impulsive than she should be, but when she loves someone—there is nothing she won't do for them, even if it hurts her own chance at happiness."

"Why are you telling me this?"

"Because I saw the way she looked at you. If she falls in love with you, make sure you are worthy of that kind of love. Colby's father took advantage of her. She doesn't need to go another round with disappointment."

The puppy had teeth.

"Is that a warning?" Jake asked in a tone that backed most men down.

Aaron removed his hand from Jake's sleeve, but did not step back. "I guess you could say that it is."

"Bold move to take with your potential new employer."

The young man adjusted his wrinkled T-shirt and said, "Some things are worth the risk."

Jake nodded. Loyalty was something he respected. "Send that resume. I think you'll do fine in the Boston office."

Aaron let out a long sigh. Not smiling. Just waiting. Even more impressive.

Jake said, "I'm only here to make sure Lil is safe. There is nothing more than that between us."

After a moment, Aaron stepped away and seemed to relax. He said, "Whatever you do, don't send her flowers. She hates watching them die. She says it's as sexy as receiving a bouquet of hamsters stapled to rulers."

Jake grimaced a bit at the image. "That's quite a visual."

Aaron said, "That's Lil. She likes images that evoke emotion. Ask her to sketch something for you sometime. She doesn't belong in an office, she belongs in a studio bringing those images to life. She'll never be happy on the path she's recently chosen for herself. If you care about her, you might want to help her see that."

A fist of fire curled deep in Jake's abdomen, but he held back further discourse. He didn't like Aaron giving him advice on how to deal with Lil. He didn't like that his displeasure was most likely obvious to the young man before him.

The entire trip was a waste of time and emotion. After today, Jake would have no reason to ever see Lil again—except perhaps across the room at a social event.

Whatever mess she got tangled up in next time would be none of his concern.

Oddly, that thought made him scowl again.

Chapter Four

L IL PULLED UP to the front of the news station. She unbuckled her seat belt and turned toward Jake. "Give me the paper." She held out her hand.

Jake took the paper out of his pocket and turned it in his hand thoughtfully. "It'd be better if you waited out here with Colby while I go in."

"Just give me that damn paper," Lil said and made a grab for it, but Jake moved it back out of her reach.

"I don't understand you, Lil. Why is it so important for you to do this? Dominic or I could have easily handled it with a phone call from New York, but you didn't take anyone's calls. I could resolve this for you right now—be back in the car in ten minutes and you wouldn't even have disturbed Colby."

"I want to fix this myself."

"That much is obvious, but I keep asking myself the same question. Why?"

Lil gestured at her baby in the back seat. "She's why. If you genuinely want to know why I'm doing what I'm doing, the answer is almost always the same. Her. She deserves the kind of stability and love that I had growing up."

"Then why won't you let Dominic help you?"

Lil threw a hand up in the air for emphasis. "You don't get it, do you? Dominic is a fantasy. Not even my fantasy—Abby's. Which is fine. She can walk away from her life and tie her happiness to the whim of some man who may or may not be there for her in a month, but I can't." Lil laid a hand on the back of her baby's car seat. "I have to think of Colby now and what's best for her."

He wasn't going to debate Dominic's loyalty—honestly, Dominic was dangerously unpredictable lately. He really couldn't say what he would be like a month from now. Was his transformation permanent or just an extreme and temporary reaction to his father's death? There was no way to know, but none of that was going to get him an insight he could use. "And dragging your daughter in there to witness something she won't remember is going to help her how?"

"It proves to me that I can do this on my own. I didn't need the support of her biological father, I don't need Abby, and I certainly don't need some New York billionaire who came here only because his boss asked him to. You want to help me? Don't stand in my way. Let me do this."

When Jake didn't immediately hand her the paper she added, "Please."

And his breath caught in his throat. The raw emotion in her explanation far outweighed any he'd expressed in perhaps his entire life. It made him want to protect her even though she was asking for him to do the exact opposite.

He handed her the paper. "I'm still coming with you,

but I won't interfere."

She studied him quietly before removing her baby from the seat behind them. "I can handle this."

He watched her stride toward the NBN Communications building, shoulders set back with determination, baby balanced on one hip and he thought he'd never seen anything more beautiful. She was a tigress going to battle for the little one in her arms.

The sight was oddly humbling—as if he were witnessing an event he'd carry with him the rest of his life.

His short reflection allowed her to reach the building before him. One step quickly became a short sprint. She wasn't going in there alone if he could help it.

LIL CHARGED THROUGH the front door of the news station and went directly to the receptionist's desk. "I want to see the station manager."

"Do you have an appointment?" The blond receptionist who appeared to have dressed for a dance club rather than her day job dismissed Lil with little more than a glance.

Lil wasn't sure if she should address her next request to the woman directly or to the abundance of cleavage threatening to burst out of her tiny top. "I—" Lil started to say, but the woman stood and flashed a huge smile at someone behind Lil.

"Mr. Walton, I'll tell Mr. Cooper that you're here," the receptionist said in a suddenly sultry voice.

Oh, please. Could she be more obvious? It wasn't amazing that she'd recognized him, anyone with a TV would have. Lil kicked herself for not thinking of that. But, seriously, did this bimbo have to throw herself at him? *I am not going to be happy if I have to stand here and watch these two hook up just so I can meet the manager.* "You should have stayed in the car," Lil hissed at Jake.

"You'd prefer to have to wait?" Jake asked.

At least he didn't appear to have any interest in the woman who was practically drooling over him. Did he meet with that kind of fawning from women wherever he went? No wonder he looked bored all the time.

I'm not here to analyze Jake's dating habits.

And he'd made a valid point. What did doing this the hard way really prove? She was being ridiculous. Still, she had come this far, she might as well follow her plan through. "Please, just let me do this my way."

"I won't say a word."

He wouldn't have to. His mere presence had already changed the rules of engagement.

The manager rushed out of his office, looking a bit ruffled. He walked right past Lil and offered his hand to Jake. "Mr. Walton, what brings you to NBN today?"

Jake ignored his outstretched hand. "I believe your business is with Miss Dartley."

The man wasn't smart enough to hide his sneer. "If you wanted to be compensated for your interview, Miss Dartley, you should have negotiated a price before giving it."

Jake took an aggressive step toward him, but Lil wasn't going to be dismissed that easily. She handed Jake both Colby and the diaper bag. She took the folded gag order out of her purse and handed it to the manager. "I didn't give an interview. The phone conversation you have was taped without my knowledge and under the guise of something else. If you or any other news station airs it, I will sue you and them to within a penny of bankruptcy."

The manager almost said something, but changed his mind. He looked back and forth between Lil and Jake, putting more meaning on their relationship than the paper in his hand.

When he spoke again, his intention was to appease her. "I had no idea, Ms. Dartley. Of course the interview will be pulled."

It was disappointingly easy.

Which shouldn't be a problem, but it was.

Today had proven nothing.

Lil turned and took Colby back from Jake. Storming out, but leaving Jake standing there with the diaper bag hanging from one of his perfectly manicured hands.

It must have provided the station manager with a sight that amused him, because the man appeared to have something he wanted to say.

Jake leaned in. "Say it. Give me one reason to remember your name when I walk out of here, and you'll spend the rest of your life wishing you hadn't."

The smile wiped clean off the older man's face, a fact that gave Jake a moment of satisfaction as he turned on his heel to do what he'd never done in his entire life—chase after a woman.

Chapter Five

BY THE TIME Jake got back to the car, Lil had already started the vehicle and Colby was safely strapped in the back. "I did it. He's not going to air it."

"You did it."

She smiled. "I really did it. I'm sure it helped that you were here, but I think it would have worked regardless."

"I bet you're right."

"You must be glad it's over. Now you can go back to New York and tell Dominic there is nothing to worry about." Lil let out a tremulous breath. "I know it's silly, but I was actually nervous in there. My legs still feel a little shaky. Adrenaline, I guess."

Jake put a hand on his seat belt and asked, "Why don't I drive?"

Lil hesitated for a moment then unbuckled hers. "Only because I'm still a little wound up."

"Of course."

They quickly traded places. As they pulled onto a main road, Jake asked, "I have to make a quick stop somewhere, do you mind?"

Although Lil wanted nothing more than to get home and relax, she said, "That's fine." He had, after all, driven all the way up here just to help her. She'd be home soon enough. Hopefully the press would be gone. If she could settle Colby down for a nap, she might even get some studying done today after all.

Lil stared blindly at the skyscrapers they drove by. Even if she didn't want to, there was something that needed to be said. "I don't think I thanked you for coming up here, Jake. I'm not really good at accepting help."

"Really, I wouldn't have guessed," he said smoothly, with only the slightest trace of humor in his voice.

Lil smiled. "Don't start with me. I'm trying to be nice."

"Is it an arduous effort?"

"With some people," Lil joked.

He seemed to want to say more, but didn't. Instead he pulled in front of a high-end residential building and handed the keys to her economy car to a valet, appearing unperturbed by the expression on the young man's face when he took them. She guessed that he didn't park many cars that smelled of baby powder and sour milk. Lil unclipped the portable section of the car seat and swung the diaper bag over one shoulder. Hopefully wherever they were headed had a spot where she could change and feed Colby or her daughter's pleasant personality would soon undergo a drastic change.

The security man at the front desk waved them by. Lil followed Jake through the pristine lobby and to an elevator that looked nice enough to live in. She wondered what kind of people lived in a place like that.

People like Jake, she guessed.

They took the elevator all the way to the top to the penthouse, not a surprise. What did give Lil a moment of pause was the way the penthouse was decorated. Large, comfortable furniture. Warm, feminine colors. It couldn't be Jake's place, could it? "Do you live here?"

"No, it belongs to a friend."

Of course it did.

He probably had a lot of friends.

A moment of jealousy was quickly followed by a mental self-shake—none of that was any of her business and she'd be a whole lot happier if she remembered that. She placed Colby's carrier on the floor and unhooked her. "Colby's wet. Do you mind if I change her on the bed? I have a blanket."

A moment later she returned from the bedroom and said, "You didn't tell me that your friend had a baby, too. The bedroom has a crib and a changing table."

Jake didn't respond to that. Instead he said, "Why don't you check out the view? It's quite impressive. You can see the Charles from the balcony."

Lil opened one of the French-style doors and gasped with pleasure. The penthouse was just high enough to give a clear view of not only the river, but a good portion of Boston. "It's beautiful."

"I'm glad you like it. That will make this easier."

The hair on the back of her neck went up.

"Make what easier?"

Jake turned, his hands casually pocketed. "You can't go

back to your place."

"No . . ." She looked around in stunned refusal.

"Yes."

"You can't—"

He motioned to the room around them with one hand. "It's already done. As you saw, you'll find that whatever you need for Colby is already here. Your personal things are being shipped over or stored as we speak."

"I already told Dominic that I wouldn't take his charity. I don't want this place."

"That was before your interview."

"I fixed that. The interview won't air."

"Lil, it's that simple. Even without airing, your interview has caught the public's attention. And that means paparazzi . . ."

"Why would people care about me? I'm not marrying a billionaire."

"No, but your sister is and that is a fact that, no matter how much you'd like to pretend it doesn't matter, does."

"I won't stay here."

"You don't have a choice." His expression hardened.

Her mouth went dry. "What does that mean?" Was he threatening her? Jake was smooth, but he was no one's lapdog. Although he deferred to Dominic, she didn't doubt that he was a force to be reckoned with on his own.

He approached her and spoke in a tone she was sure he used during his business negotiations. "It means it's the only course of action that makes sense and you'll see that once you calm down."

Of course he wasn't threatening her—he'd have to muster up enough emotion to do that.

Lashing out, she said, "Really? Once I calm down? Forgive me for having an emotional response to manipulation. Sorry that unlike you I don't blindly follow Dominic's orders. We're not all his puppets."

Lil felt a slight triumph as her barb brought a flush to his cheeks. Still, his voice remained maddeningly even and rational. "Luckily, your opinion of me has nothing to do with the outcome of this situation. You'll stay here, not because Dominic told you to and not because I told you to; you'll stay because you and your daughter are no longer safe at your old house. If what you said earlier is true and you do base all of your decisions on her welfare, then you'll accept this as necessary."

How easily he threw her words back at her.

Lil hugged Colby closer. *Stuff like this didn't really happen, did it?* "There has to be another way. What if I said yes to temporary security?"

He shook his head calmly. "You'll have security here."

"You can't do this," she said desperately.

"It's done," he replied with a finality she couldn't accept.

"I can't believe Abby went along with this! How could she think she could just spring this on me and I'd be okay with it?"

He shrugged. "She may not know I'm here."

"So, this isn't even her idea? It's her crazy lover's? But why send you? Anyone could have broken the bad news to me." The answer came to her with sickening clarity. "Oh, wait, you're the fixer, right? That's what Abby told me. Dominic breaks all the rules and then sends you in to smooth it over. I'm just a problem he sent you to fix." She hated that her accusation ended with what sounded suspiciously like a sob.

Jake approached, his expression softening with concern. "Lil . . ."

She put a hand up to stop him. *Oh, no, pity would only make this worse.* "No, don't say anything else. I get it. Excuse me."

Dominic had sent his right-hand man. *I must be a bigger screwup than I know.* Lil picked up the diaper bag and headed back toward the bedroom. She needed a moment to collect her thoughts, to take all of this in. She sat on the edge of the bed and absently offered Colby one of her snacks and a bottle of formula.

After satisfying her immediate needs, Colby fell asleep in Lil's lap. Lil crossed the room and tucked her into the white crib. It was obviously an expensive one and whoever had set up the room had taken the time to add a mobile that matched the one hanging above her crib in Lil's home. Abby knew about this penthouse. She might not know about today's bait and switch, but she'd definitely played a part in decorating these rooms. Her soft, maternal touch was evident in all of them.

Some of Lil's anger dissipated. She couldn't really blame them for thinking she needed to be protected—contained.

She looked down at her daughter and thought, *So much has changed, and nothing has really changed at all.*

But it will, Colby.
It will.

JAKE WAS SEATED on the flower-print couch when Lil returned to the living room. He stood as soon as he saw her.

Neither said anything at first.

Lil broke the awkward silence. "Do you really think we're in danger?"

Jake loosened his tie as if he suddenly found it a bit constricting. "Dominic has as many enemies as he has allies and it only takes one."

Lil spoke, scanning the main area of the penthouse. "How long will it take for this to pass over? Surely people will forget about me when the next story catches their attention."

"There is no going back. The sooner you accept that your life has changed, the easier it will be on you and Colby." The even tone of Jake's voice grated.

Some of Lil's anger returned. "How can you say it like that? I didn't choose this. I don't want this."

He stood and approached her calmly. "What do you want me to say, Lil?"

She flung angry words at him. "I want you to look like you care that this is ruining everything for me. How am I going to take my final exam tomorrow? I can't even get out of my driveway . . . oh, wait, I don't have a driveway anymore. Just this . . . this . . ." She waved her hand around referencing the penthouse.

He stood above her, sending her hormones into overdrive. Her body wasn't concerned with why they were there, it tensed and tingled. His eyes dilated and his breathing changed to match her own. Without touching, they synchronized on a level that was foreign to both of them. In that moment, there was no yesterday, no tomorrow—just two people fighting off an attraction that defied what either of them thought they wanted.

He groaned and slid a hand beneath her hair, cupping her head, and pulling her to him. He kissed her with an unexpected flood of passion; a passion her body leapt to match.

It was not the timid kiss of one who was testing a new flavor, but rather the bold claiming by a man who had tasted and returned with a hunger. Lil closed her eyes and lost herself in a wave of pleasure. His other hand slid across her backside, lifting her against him. Her skirt bunched beneath the strong hand that held her, kneading her ass through the cotton material.

He pulled back slightly. "We can't do this," he said, his hot breath warming her lips.

She looked up at him, desire impairing her ability to provide a witty comeback. Her body was sending wild sensations from every area their bodies touched. She wanted, needed, to feel more of him.

"I meant what I said about anything between us being a bad idea," he said huskily.

His words doused the heat within her. She tore herself out of his embrace and adjusted her skirt. "Then you seriously have to stop kissing me," she said angrily.

He ran a frustrated hand through his hair, mussing it the way she would have gladly done had he not been such a jackass.

He said, "Obviously, there is a certain amount of attraction between the two of us."

"But you think Dominic won't approve?" she goaded. She wanted to hurt him as he was hurting her.

"I don't care what Dominic thinks, but one of us has to stay focused on—" He stopped himself.

"On?" She put a hand on her hip and waited.

"Business. Just business. Listen—" he started.

She cut him off. "No, you listen. Why are you messing around with my head today? This whole forced move has done enough of that, thank you. I've got an exam tomorrow morning that I'm probably going to fail because I should have been studying today, but I already blew that. If I can figure out how to get my hands on my books, I might be able to use this time while Colby is napping—not that I'll be able to concentrate after this." When he looked like he was about to say something Lil held up a hand and said, "Please don't explain again why we can't be together. I've heard just about enough of that. Just leave."

Jake paced restlessly before her and ran his hand through his hair again. "You're hurt."

Lil snorted. "You're delusional. Sure, you're sexy and rich and women probably fall at your feet all the time, but to hurt me, I would have to care about you, which I don't. Whatever attraction you feel—ignore it. That's what I'm doing."

He looked a bit bemused.

She stopped and shook her head. "You stopped listening at sexy, didn't you?"

A slight flush spread across his cheeks. "I've tried to ignore it," he said softly.

She folded her arms protectively across her chest.

He moved closer and ran his hands from her tense shoulders, down her arms and pulled her gently toward him. "You're not my type," he said almost to himself.

She stubbornly kept her arms folded, even as his hands slid lower and encircled her waist.

"You're definitely not mine, either," she replied. "You're way too uptight."

He eased her against him again and said, "You're far too unpredictable."

Her body tightened and quivered. She met his eyes boldly. "You never listen."

A half smile curled the corner of his mouth. "You never shut up."

Time stood still and the air around them sizzled. She bit her bottom lip as the tension mounted and she gave in to the temptation to feel him against her. Sliding her arms up and around his neck, she fit perfectly against him and his mounting excitement. "So, we agree."

With one strong move, he lifted her at her waist, rubbing her deliciously against him. "Yes." He swung her higher, forcing her to wrap her legs around him to steady herself. With one step, she was partially seated on the table behind the couch. He tossed a decorative bowl onto the cushions below and rested her more fully there, exploring her mouth with his while his hands slid beneath her skirt and followed her long legs down to remove her shoes with a flip.

Strong hands ran up and down the length of her legs as if he could not get enough of her, as if he were memorizing every curve and corner of her. His kisses moved from her mouth to her neck. Exploring. Tasting. His hot breath licking at her. She steadied herself with her hands on his shoulders.

He spread her legs further apart and slid a finger beneath the silk of her panties and between her eager folds. With painstaking thoroughness, he explored and caressed. When he found the spot that made her shudder against him, he lavished it with attention. Each stroke increased the building heat within her. She wanted to feel him inside her, claiming her.

She squirmed against his hand, leaning back as her excitement replaced coherent thought. He filled her center first with one finger and then as she welcomed that with a moan, he inserted another and moved back and forth within her. Lil cried out as the pleasure became more than she could contain.

She nearly wept in protest when his kisses and his hands stopped simultaneously.

He eased her further back and slid her panties out from beneath her. With another deft move, her skirt was bunched around her waist, her bare ass exposed to the cold of the table and her warm center once again opened to his attentive fingers.

In her growing desperation to feel him, she pulled his

shirt out from his pants and slid her hands up his rock-hard abdomen, enjoying the feel of his muscles clenching beneath her touch. One of his hands held her head firmly in place while his lips plundered, his tongue circling and teasing hers, while his other hand tickled her outer folds until she was spreading her legs wider for him, begging him to once again use his thumb and magical fingers on her. He did and she was soon jutting against his hand, writhing in pleasure.

She slumped a bit when he removed both hands for a moment and almost came when he tore the front of her shirt open with one powerful move. He pushed one cup of her bra aside and licked her puckered nipple, lapping and nipping at it softly until Lil was moaning and yanking off what was left of her shirt, tossing her bra onto the floor silently begging him to give her other breast equal attention.

Which he did.

She leaned back onto her hands while he continued to worship her with his lips, his tongue, and those wildly knowledgeable fingers. He pushed her gently back until she was fully reclined against the back cushion of the couch and stood above her for a moment.

Then he bent to taste her and she closed her eyes and rode the explosion of heat that rushed through her body. He licked the exposed area of her stomach, the sensitive flesh of her inner thighs and then his tongue followed the path his fingers had. She dug her hands into the fabric on either side of her head, unsure if she could stop herself from begging him to enter her.

She heard the crisp sound of his zipper opening quickly

followed by the tear of a condom package and her excitement heightened tenfold.

Take me, she thought feverishly. *Take me now.*

He wrapped an arm beneath her waist and hauled her up until she was eye to eye with him, the material of his unremoved pants rubbing against the inside of her thighs. Her hands gripped his shoulders through his jacket and she closed her eyes in anticipation.

"Look at me," he growled.

And she did. She looked into those hot, golden eyes as she felt his tip tease her wetness. A gasp escaped her when he filled her with one powerful move. Her body naturally clenched around him and they began to move in union. He gripped her hips and positioned her so he could go deeper.

Never breaking rhythm, he explored her from within, adjusting and seeking until each stroke sent a shudder of pleasure through her. She gripped at the smooth material of his shirt, pulling him back down to take her breasts into his mouth once again.

His mouth returned to hers and their climaxes were shared, all consuming, and left them both shuddering against each other.

He stepped back and offered her his hand in a gentlemanly move that seemed ridiculously out of place in the scene. She took it only because she suddenly felt overexposed lying there, quickly breaking contact to reach down for her shirt. When she looked up from securing it the best she could around her and adjusting her skirt, he was already perfectly put together again. If she could ignore the residual throbbing of pleasure between her legs or the places her body was still warm from his touch, it would have been easy to believe she had imagined the entire interlude. Unfortunately, the panties and bra that taunted her from behind him were indeed hers.

"Lil, I—"

She brushed past him and hastily bent to snatch the offending articles of clothing off the floor and stuff them behind the cushion of the couch. What could he say? Nothing she wanted to hear. "Don't say anything." She held the front of her shirt closed with one hand and pointed to the door with her other. "Just go."

Looking much more miserable than any man should after sharing what Lil considered the best sex in her limited experience, he said, "This was . . ."

"A mistake," Lil ended his sentence for him. "You don't have to say it. You don't have to try to sugarcoat this with sweet words. I'm not naive. I know it doesn't mean anything."

"Don't . . ."

"Don't what? Don't say the truth? Don't acknowledge what we're both thinking? Look me in the eye and tell me you don't want to run out that door and forget this ever happened."

He couldn't.

"Go, Jake. Go back to New York. I'll be fine. This was a mistake that we'd be better off pretending didn't happen."

He walked to the door and shook his head. "I don't make mistakes like this."

"Well, welcome to the human race," Lil said and slammed the door.

Chapter Six

JAKE RODE DOWN in the elevator, chastising himself as he went. He was not an impulsive man. Life was a game best played like chess—each move only undertaken after all the possible outcomes had been considered.

Something inexplicable happened to that belief when he came within a certain proximity to one outspoken, fiery brunette. Half the time he wasn't sure if he was insulted, irritated, turned-on or some bizarre combination of all three.

Now he was in the unique position of being thoroughly confused.

It wasn't until he stepped onto the curb that he remembered he had driven Lil's car. Instinctively, he dialed the number of someone who was technically Dominic's personal assistant, but had become so much more than that to both of them over the years. He had yet to find a crisis Mrs. Duhamel didn't take in stride.

"Marie, I'm at Lil Dartley's place. I need a . . ."

The older woman interrupted his request. "She moved in?"

"Yes, she and Colby are settling in, but since we drove

her car here this morning . . ."

"How did she take it? Was she upset?"

"She was . . ." *Fantastic! That's the problem.*

Oh, hell, what was he supposed to say to the woman who was closer to being a mother figure to him than his own mother ever had been? "She was angry at first. Then . . ." He didn't mean for it to happen, but his frustration spilled forth. "It's ridiculous for me to even be here. This isn't my problem; it's Dominic's. His family, his issue. Have my helicopter readied and at my Cambridge office building. I'll be flying back in about an hour. I'll also need a car to pick me up. I left mine at Lil's house."

"You didn't line up transportation back? That's not like you," Marie asked with surprise.

Jake turned his back so his comment wouldn't be heard by the valet who was hovering and snapped, "I can't make a mistake? Will the world end if I slip up even once?"

"What's really bothering you, Jake?"

With a sigh, Jake said tiredly, "Nothing. Just send a car."

"Is it Lil? Did you two have a fight? Maybe you should stay and try to work it out instead of coming back to New York."

Calling Marie had been a mistake. He wasn't ready to discuss the jumble of emotions coursing through him. "I didn't call you for a lecture."

Her tone softened and had she been there she probably would have offered him something to eat. When either he or Dominic got particularly abrupt with her, she often tried to soothe their mood with food. Sometimes it worked. Lacking that option, she was employing the supportive, maternal voice—her other secret weapon. "You didn't call me for a car, either. You have the Boston car service on speed dial. You and Dominic are so much alike . . ."

Jake made a sound in his throat. "I cannot imagine two people more different than Dom and me."

Marie laughed softly and said, "Really? Do you know that he called me the night he met Abby?"

"This is an entirely different situation."

"Jake, it's me, Marie. I know you well enough to know when you have something you want to tell me."

Jake loosened his tie and took off his jacket. The midday sun was baking him in his dark suit and was the reason for his foul mood—the only reason he was willing to acknowledge. "Coming here was a bad idea, Marie. Just a bad idea."

"Oh, my God. You slept with her."

He didn't say a word.

"Jake! Well, there is no way you are coming home tonight. What were you thinking?" she asked. He imagined the disappointment in her eyes and scowled.

I wasn't.

Jake didn't have to answer. Marie continued on. "You turn yourself around, Jake, and you go back in there and make sure that girl is okay."

He felt about five years old when she used that tone with him. "I can't do that."

"You can and you will." Steel entered the older woman's voice. "I don't care what happened between the two of you today; she's a single mother. You were supposed to make sure she was settled in. Did you check to see if the groceries had arrived? Do you know if she needs anything?"

"No," he admitted and felt more like a heel with each word Marie threw at him. He sighed, rubbing his forehead. "Why did I call you again?"

Her tone softened. "Because you knew you were wrong, but you needed someone to say it."

He half laughed in self-deprecation. "She's going to think I'm crazy when I knock on the door now."

"Do you remember that time Dominic sent you into the Republic of Dabron to talk them into honoring their contract even as their government was under attack by rebel leaders? I asked you if you were afraid—"

This was not the time to reminisce. "I don't see what that has to do with this situation."

Marie corrected him gently. "You said, 'Fear is the first guest you should uninvite to any party.'"

"I'm not—" He stopped mid-denial.

Damn.

He could handle rebel leaders. He could talk his way around irate dictators. For the right incentive, he could even negotiate a lucrative truce between two governments that were out to destroy each other. There was something invigorating about bringing order and calm to where there had been none.

Lil was different.

She scared him because around her, *he* was the chaos.

"Dominic sent me to make sure she was safe, Marie."

Fine job I did of that.

With a wry tone of humor, Marie responded, "Painful as the revelation is, Jake, you're not perfect. That doesn't mean that you shouldn't fix this situation, though. Lil just had a new life dumped on her. Imagine how lost she must feel."

"I already feel badly about how I behaved."

"So, what are you going to do about it?"

What can I do?

Before the question was even completed in his mind, an idea came to him.

He hung up, turned around and headed back into the building.

He knew exactly how to make this right.

Chapter Seven

L IL HEARD THE knock on the door and wondered if such a place had room service. Maybe some of her things had arrived? She secured her jacket over her now button-free shirt. A quick look in the hallway mirror confirmed her fear that her hair was tumbling down out of its bun and her face was still flushed from sex.

Well, not too much I can do about either.

She opened the door and almost slammed it shut. It was Jake, jacket flung over one shoulder, looking a bit more disheveled than she remembered from just a short while ago.

"May I come in?" he asked politely as if they hadn't recently engaged in wild, animalistic table sex.

"I don't think it's a good idea," she said, holding the door firmly in one hand to block his entry.

"We need to talk," he said bluntly.

Au contraire.

"I think we said everything that needed to be said." She went to close the door, but he moved one foot forward and blocked it from fully closing.

"I didn't."

"Don't make this ugly, Jake."

He gave her that bland look that she was learning meant that regardless of what she said he was going to wait out the situation and then do as he pleased.

With a sigh of resignation, she swung the door open. How much worse could today get? "Oh, come on in."

Barefoot, she led the way to the living room and sat on one of the oversized chairs; he sat on the couch across from her. The silence was heavy and prolonged.

He cleared his throat. "So you have everything you need for Colby?"

"Yes," Lil said slowly.

"And the pantry is properly stocked?"

Lil shook her head in confusion. What was he doing? She defaulted to sarcasm. "I have no idea. I haven't gotten much farther than the couch."

His face reddened ever so slightly, but he didn't counter. Instead, he stood and crossed to the refrigerator and then the cabinets, opening and closing each. "Your books will arrive in twenty minutes along with some clothes, but the rest of your things will be delivered tomorrow so you won't be disturbed tonight."

"Thank you?" The stilted and superficial conversation between them felt a bit surreal. Where was the man who had torn her shirt off with one lustful move?

He returned to the living room area, looking unsure if he wanted to sit down or pace the room. "Your car is still valet parked in the garage. You'll have a choice tomorrow morning of taking it or calling for a driver. I left the number with the front desk. They know to have a car seat for you."

"It wasn't necessary . . ."

"It's what I came here for."

Well, that stung.

Lil stood and took a step toward the door. "Of course. Well, then, thank you and I'm fine now. You can go back and tell Dominic that you fulfilled your task."

Instead of responding to her jab, he said, "So, you have an exam tomorrow morning?"

"Yes," she replied, wondering where this conversation was going.

"I contacted the nanny you've used before. She should be here in an hour. That should allow you to study tonight." Wow, Jake thought of everything. Too bad leaving so she could start pretending today had never happened had not yet occurred to him.

She had to admit that getting her a babysitter for the night was thoughtful. Not that she wanted to see him as anything but an arrogant, controlling ass, but having someone there that night would help her. *Wait.* "And she was available? She was good; I would have thought she'd have another position."

"She did, but she was willing to leave it. The service found a replacement for her."

"Just like that?" Did anyone say no to Jake?

"Everyone has a price."

What an awful and absolutely untrue way to view people.

She put her hands on her hips. "I don't and I'm not comfortable with a nanny who can be bought, either."

His eyebrows rose in recognition of her point. "I'll cancel her and have the service send someone else." He took out his phone.

Lil shook her head and reached out to stop him, pulling back just before she touched him. "No, I'll see who I can find. I might have to drop Colby off, but I have friends who will help me on short notice."

"I'll watch her."

Whoa. Just whoa. "What?"

One of his eyebrows rose as if to say that she had heard him perfectly well and he didn't appreciate repeating himself. "I'm already here; it makes sense for me to do it—unless you're not comfortable with me watching her either."

"You're serious."

"I don't joke much."

No kidding.

He couldn't seriously be offering to watch her daughter while she studied, could he? He was a billionaire, a man in charge of countless companies. He didn't get to where he was by hanging around. Was he hoping she'd sleep with him again? If so, he was sure going about it in an odd way.

"Colby is going to wake up hungry," she said, testing his offer.

"I'm sure you can direct me to the necessary supplies."

"And wet." When he said nothing, she added, "You might have to change her diaper."

The frustratingly even-tempered Jake had returned. He didn't so much as bat an eyelash at the possibility. "You'll be here. Shown once, I'm sure I'll be able to handle subsequent changes. How old is she?"

"Six months old."

He typed something into his phone.

"Are you looking up how to care for a six-month-old?"

A slight flush spread across his cheeks. He sounded a bit defensive when he said, "Information gleaned from the Internet has a high reliability of accuracy if cross-referenced with at least three reputable sites." He paused his search for a moment. "How much longer do you think she will sleep?"

"Maybe twenty minutes more? Her normal nap is two hours."

"Great," he said, throwing his jacket across the back of the couch and settling himself back onto its thick cushions. "By then I'll be a pro. Set up her things over here and you can use that table." He pointed to the one in the adjoining dining area.

"Sure," Lil said and felt a bit like she must be dreaming. She gathered Colby's toss blanket and a few of her toys and set up an area on the floor near Jakes feet. She also readied a bottle. The main desk rang up to say that a few boxes were being sent up. Lil spread her books across the table and looked across the room at Jake who was still reading something on his phone.

A wail from the bedroom announced the end of Colby's nap and the smell that assailed Lil's nostrils when she entered the room almost convinced her to change Colby in the bedroom, but then a wicked thought came to her and she brought the diaper bag and changing pad with her to the living room instead.

Let's see what Jake is really made of.

She chose an area on the floor just past the blanket she'd put down earlier for her daughter. Lil positioned herself on the opposite side of Colby.

Jake put his phone down, his expression devoid of the distaste she'd expected.

Taking nothing for granted, she explained each step from wipe to paste, periodically peering up expecting a reaction that never came.

He simply asked, "Do you use the paste every time?"

Lil closed and adjusted the new diaper and placed the soiled one in a sealable, disposable baggie. "She is just starting with cereal and snacks, so I do right now. I didn't have to as much when she was only on formula."

Positioning Colby in the middle of the blanket with some toys, Lil gathered up the supplies and went to wash her hands in the kithchen.

On her return, she saw Jake lean down and move a toy just beyond Colby's reach. He must have seen the question in her eyes, because he said, "Research says that if you place things just out of a baby's reach, they are more motivated to move. It also lays a foundation for problem solving."

Emotion constricted Lil's vocal cords, making a nod her only response. She wanted to hate Jake or at least to find a reason to dislike him. *Dear universe, you already tempted me with him and I failed your test—must you rub it in?*

Lil returned from the kitchen with a bottle and a towel for Jake's shoulder. She was going to hand Colby to him, but he moved down onto the floor and rested his back against the front of the couch. He lifted Colby easily until she was eye to eye with him and said, "I will pay you a thousand dollars if you don't spit up on me."

Colby grabbed his nose and pulled. He smiled and said, "You're a hard bargainer, but you won't get a penny more." He settled her into the crook of one arm and held up a hand to receive the bottle from Lil.

Lil knew her mouth was open in the most unflattering way, but she couldn't help it. She handed him both the bottle and the towel. He placed the towel over one shoulder like he'd done it a hundred times before.

"Do you have children?" she asked.

He shook his head and looked down at Colby who was now happily guzzling her formula. "No, but I have friends who do."

"And you babysat for them?"

He shuddered. "God no, I don't like children."

Colby twisted his bottom lip between her little fingers. He pulled back to escape the pinch, but didn't look bothered. When Lil continued to stand over him—staring, he said, "Go study."

As she headed across the room, she heard Jake say to Colby, "I don't do peek-a-boo even if it's developmentally appropriate for you. However, when you finish your bottle, we can look at your toy portfolio and determine if it is adequately diverse."

Impossible as the task appeared at first, Lil lost herself in her class notes and test prep questions, allowing herself no more than quick glances to ensure that Colby and Jake were still fine. After the first run through, she made the mistake of allowing her attention to linger on them.

Colby was on her stomach on her throw blanket and Jake was seated next to it, talking in that even tone. Lil only caught a word here and there—all of which sounded like he was explaining investment strategies, but since her daughter appeared to be enjoying the undivided attention of an adult, Lil didn't comment on his choice of discourse.

"I don't like kids," he'd said.

Oh, how much easier all of this would be if that were true.

Jake didn't know it yet, but one day he was going to be a wonderful father to some lucky woman's child.

Just not mine.

Lil stood and closed her book. She was as ready as she'd ever be. Time to release Jake from his obligation. Walking over, Lil picked her daughter up and cuddled her against her chest. "Thank you," she said.

Jake slowly unfolded himself from the floor and stood, stretching when he reached his full height. "Did you get everything done that you wanted to?"

"Yes."

Jake stretched again and reached for his jacket. With quick precision, he adjusted his clothing, tightened his tie, and ran a smoothing hand through his slightly disheveled hair. In a matter of moments, he was back—the perfectly groomed, perfectly in control man whose mere existence made her a bit defensive.

He handed her a card. "If you need help for tomorrow morning, call this number."

It was the nanny service.

"I should be fine. I lined up a sitter a while ago."

"Yes, of course. Then I should be going." He looked around as if assuring himself that there was nothing left undone. Their eyes met and for just a split second Lil thought she saw a spark of desire in their dark depths, but it passed and might easily have only been in her imagination. "A limo will come for you on Friday. A jet will take you and Colby to a private airport in New York."

Her heart missed a beat.

Was it possible that he was inviting her to join him in New York?

She couldn't do that.

She shouldn't do that.

But for just a moment, she wanted to agree to go wherever he wanted to take her.

What am I saying? She gave herself a mental shake.

Jake said, "Dominic and your sister are having a large party this weekend. They said it was important for you to attend."

Lil's stomach lurched painfully and she bit her lip to hold in her thoughts.

Dominic and Abby.

Of course.

"I'll think about it." She walked with him to the door. *Please just leave.*

"I believe it's related to their engagement. This is one you shouldn't miss."

A part of her wanted to believe that he was saying that because he wanted to see her again. *Don't be a fool.* She asked sarcastically, "So, Dominic told you to make sure I went?"

The slight incline of his head was all the acknowledgement she required.

I might be sick now.

"Goodbye, Jake." Baby in one arm, she held the door open with her other.

He stepped through the doorway and paused. "You were right, Lil. This afternoon doesn't have to change anything. We're going to see each other at events. It doesn't have to be awkward."

Sure, only listen when I'm talking out my ass.

She closed the door in his face and leaned her back against it. Looking down at her daughter, she said, "Don't look at me like that. I know he's not coming back. I'm just being stupid now so that I'll be more sympathetic when you're older and dating."

Colby smiled.

"I know. I like him, too." Lil pushed away from the door and carried her daughter back into the living room, their new living room.

Another day, another story I can't share with Abby.

LATER THAT NIGHT, back in his home, Jake sent Dominic a quick text. "It's done. She's in her new place. Meet tomorrow morning?"

Dominic replied, "Can't. Sent a packet to your office regarding the party though."

"And the two people you'd like me to meet?"

"They will be there Saturday."

"Did you send me their names?"

Dominic typed, "Sorry. Bad connection. Talk later."

Bad connection? More like bad joke. Why wouldn't Dominic want him to know who he'd found to work on their server? They didn't have time for surprises.

Pacing his living room, Jake ran through a mental list of all of the potential mistakes Dominic could be making. If he'd reached into the criminal world for assistance, they might end up with an altogether different problem. He hoped that this time Dominic was going to choose a solution that was less dangerous than the problem at hand.

Coming slowly to a halt, Jake took in his surroundings. Nothing had changed since he left that morning. His tablet was still positioned near the chair he reclined in each evening to read the news. Everything was still perfectly in place. His home was immaculate, contemporary, and quiet.

Empty.

Private, he corrected.

Orderly.

He thought about the chaotic evening he'd spent with the Andrades at Dominic's request. Children everywhere. Competing conversations so loud they made intelligent conversation difficult. It had been a relief to return home afterward.

He should feel the same way tonight after the roller

coaster of a day with Lil and an evening of watching her child. It bothered him that he didn't.

Instead, the day had left him feeling . . .

He dismissed the first word that came to mind since it likely had more to do with fatigue than anything else.

He was not and had never been—*lonely*.

Chapter Eight

THE NEXT DAY, Lil deposited her purse, diaper bag and notebook on the dining room table with relief and stepped out of her uncomfortable pumps. She put Colby's car seat on the floor beside the table and bent to release her, noting how her child filled it. "You are almost too big for this, Colby. Don't grow up too fast, baby."

Colby reached for her mother's hair and gave a yank, making no such promises.

Lil hugged her little one to her then held her back so she could see her beautiful face. She touched one of the blond curls. Colby smiled and the weight of everything dissolved. All of this was worth it as long as her daughter was happy and healthy. The rest would work itself out.

"Well, hopefully Mommy passed her exam this morning and can get a real job now. When I do, you're going to have to go to day care, Colby. It's not going to be easy on either one of us, but I'll find a good one and you'll get to meet other children. You might even like it."

Colby didn't understand what she was saying, and Lil was happy about that. Thus far, she'd only chosen jobs that had allowed her to work only a couple of hours a day so she could spend more time with Colby; Abby or a friend had watched her when Lil had attended night classes. She'd doubled up on her course load at times so she could get her degree earlier, but now she wished she hadn't. Things were about to change, and she wasn't sure she was ready. Most likely, she'd work an eight- to ten-hour day depending on where she found employment. An administrative assistant had to be flexible and available to work the hours her boss required. It wasn't going to be easy and it certainly wasn't her dream job, but if she wanted to build a secure future for herself and her daughter—it would require some sacrifice.

None of her sketches had made it over in the move, and that was probably for the best. It was time to let go of her childhood fantasies and put all of her energy into more practical endeavors. Maybe if she had made better choices, worked harder to get scholarships or minded her own business more—maybe she would have gone to that art school and taken her modest raw talent and done something amazing with it. Looking back and wondering what might have been was a waste of time. Growing up was about realizing that what you want to do and what you have to do are often two very different things.

Like living in an apartment paid for by your sister's lover.

A knock on the door interrupted her self-lecture.

Don't let it be Jake.

Okay, please let it be Jake.

No, I'm not ready to see him again.

Lil opened the door and told herself that she wasn't disappointed to see her friend, Alethea. As usual, Alethea was dressed in what she liked to call "casual chic." Her clothes were trendy, but low-key, the kind most people wouldn't remember later—tan cotton pants, a peach silk blouse. The only hint of the wild personality that lay beneath her deliberately bland attire stuck out from beneath her long pants; Alethea had a weakness for outrageously priced high heels.

Looking at her perfectly polished friend now, it was hard to believe they had ever stayed up all night eating pizza and watching horror movies together. Alethea's long red hair was held back in a stylish ponytail that emphasized her delicate facial features and green eyes that Lil had spent half of her life envying.

She swept into Lil's penthouse, scanning the place quickly before turning back to Lil and saying, "How is my favorite baby?"

Lil held Colby out for Alethea to take and cringed when her friend tossed her up into the air, sending the baby into a fit of giggles. When Colby's amusement subsided, Alethea tossed her again and joined the laughter.

"Please don't drop her," Lil warned.

Her friend rolled her eyes dramatically and said to Colby, "Your mother is a worry wart now. You did that to her." She wagged a finger in front of the laughing baby, tickling her with the finger and saying, "Who did it? You did it, little blondie."

Lil led the way back to the seating area. As expected, Alethea went on a quick self-guided tour, returning to join

Lil in the living room. She sat on one of the overstuffed chairs and bounced Colby on her knees. "Whew! It was actually difficult to get in here."

Lil tucked her feet beneath her on her own chair, feeling the pinch of her pencil skirt and deliberately ignoring the discomfort. "Did you try ringing up from the front desk?"

"What fun would that have been?" Alethea made a face at Colby, laughing along with the child. "Do you know you have your own personal security detail in the back alley?"

"Apparently not very good security, if you got past them."

"I haven't met a security system yet that could keep me out." Although Alethea was answering Lil's questions, she was doing so in an exaggerated tone that sent Colby back into giggles.

"Have you forgotten . . ." Lil said.

"That was high school, Lil. I hadn't realized my potential." At Lil's sour expression, she said, "Don't make me apologize for it again. Geez, you get your friend arrested one time and they hold it against you forever."

Laughing would only encourage her. Lil adjusted her position in her chair as one of her legs went numb. "I really wish you had gotten into the FBI. You need to be monitored."

"They didn't think they could reform me, but don't worry, I'm making much more money freelancing my skills. So, what happened to you? Were you snatched from your house in the middle of the day and didn't think it's worth calling me about?"

Lil smoothed the hem of her skirt down to buy some time. "I wasn't snatched," she hedged.

"Seriously, are you under some sort of home arrest?"

Although she was tempted to say yes, she grudgingly admitted, "No, Dominic is worried that Colby and I might be in danger since my interview stirred up so much interest with the press." Lil shuddered.

Her friend didn't look surprised. "He's right. Your face is everywhere right now. And your sister really could not have picked a more high-profile boyfriend."

"But I'm not . . ."

"It doesn't matter if you have money. It would be the potential of what you'd be worth to Dominic."

Lil imagined what he must have thought of her to send Jake to fix her. "This week, I'm sure that's not very much."

Alethea rolled her eyes. "I would have brought wine if I had known this was going to be a pity party. You know I hate it when you martyr out on me."

Lil glared at her as you can only openly do at someone you've been best friends with for more than a decade.

Alethea was not concerned. "Glare all you want, but I'm likely to be the only one who won't clock you in the head if you try to say how horrible it is to be forced into a life of luxury and leisure. How will you survive with around the clock maid service and an uptown address? *No, no, I want to pay my own college loans off. You can't make me take your money, Dominic.*" Alethea mimicked Lil's voice in the most unflattering way.

"Shut up. It's not like that." Lil smacked her hand down

on the arm of her chair.

Alethea just met her eyes without a word.

Lil said, "Okay, I can see how this would look wonderful to some people, but I don't want to owe anyone anything anymore. I'm so tired of being the one who doesn't know, who can't know, who everyone thinks can't survive on their own. I've made mistakes. And I'm still making mistakes." The memory of how easily she had fallen into Jake's arms made her almost as uncomfortable as the realization that she longed for something more serious with him. She continued on, her pitch rising with each word. "*Huge* stupid mistakes. I admit it. But this doesn't have to be me. I can change."

At the show of emotion, Alethea sat forward. "What did you do?"

"Nothing," Lil said and blinked back tears of frustration. Unsure if she could admit the fullness of her folly to even her closest friend.

"You might as well tell me now," Alethea said, grinning. "You know I've studied Bauer interrogation techniques. I'm not afraid to use them on you."

"Sometimes you scare me a little, Al."

Her friend only laughed. "Spill it."

Lil let her head drop back to the cushion behind her head. "I slept with Jake."

One of Alethea's hands shot skyward. "Hallelujah!"

Lil peeked out from beneath her mostly closed eyelids. "How can you say that?"

"Let's see. My best friend gets dumped over a year ago by an asshole. She swears off men and goes from being someone who enjoys a good adventure now and then to a complete and miserable stick in the mud. The universe sends her not only one of the hottest men on the planet, but also one of the richest and she takes advantage of the opportunity. Yeah, I can see how bad I'm supposed to feel for you." Alethea's sarcasm was replaced by amusement. "At least tell me he was awful in bed."

Lil blushed at the memory. "We didn't make it to the bed."

Alethea nodded and joked, "Okay, now I might hate you a little bit." Her tone turned serious again. "Lil, you really need to lighten up and enjoy the ride."

"Oh, I did," Lil drawled and the two shared a laugh.

"Now, there is the Lil I know."

Lil raised her head and both her eyebrows at that. "Are you calling me a slut?"

Her friend's response was thick with sarcasm. "Yeah, because sleeping with two guys by the age of twenty-five is everyone's definition of a whore." Her tone grew more serious. "Besides, who would care if you were one? Slut, whore . . . those are just words men use to judge what they cannot control. And, more specifically, they were the words your ex used when you proved to him that you could survive when he left you. Don't let him have any place in your head."

Lil left her seat to join Alethea on hers and simply hugged her. She really should have called her last night instead of spending hours chasing her own thoughts around. Al always knew just what to say. What's better than a friend who knows all the ugly corners of your soul and loves you anyway?

Alethea hugged her back and then said, "So, details, details."

Lil shrugged. "It was good, but it doesn't really matter. It won't happen again. I'm not his type."

"Apparently."

"No, seriously, we agreed that it was a mistake."

Alethea shook her head in mock sadness. "You mean you said it first."

Lil held her fear in. *He would have said it if I'd waited.* Sometimes the anticipation was worse than the actual desertion.

"Well, what did he say?" her friend prompted.

"He agreed that it was a mistake."

"And then?"

"And then he left."

One line appeared on Alethea's forehead, a sign that she found something puzzling. "And you haven't seen him since?"

Lil looked away. "He came back, made sure I had groceries and watched Colby so I could study for my exam."

Alethea barked out a laugh. "Wow, he sounds like such a jerk. You are so right to feel bad about the whole experience."

Lil didn't expect her friend to understand. Alethea was used to getting any man she wanted. "He only came back because Dominic had asked him to make sure I had settled in."

"Yeah, probably. Not because he's hot for you and wanted to see you again."

"It's not like that, Alethea."

Alethea turned Colby around on her lap and started bouncing her again. "Lil, I get why you are like you are. Your parents left you, Asshole left you, now you feel like your sister left you. You don't want to care because you're afraid this guy will leave you, too. I get it. But while you wallow in all that fear, you're missing out on some life changing opportunities."

"I have to be more careful. I have Colby to think of . . ."

"I respect that, but don't you think that you've whipped yourself enough for one mistake?"

Lil was instantly furious. "She is not a mistake."

Alethea smiled and handed Colby back to Lil. "Exactly. Remember that." She stood and tucked her blouse pristinely back into her slacks. "Well, I'm off to test the security system for a new optical fiber laser company. I got the contract through that guy you referred to me. Thanks."

Lil stood. "Alethea? Wait. Abby is having a huge party this weekend in New York and she wants me to go."

"Why does this sound like a question? You know you should."

It wasn't easy to admit the truth, but Lil was nervous about the party. First, she didn't think she could face Jake alone again. Second, what did she know about high-class events? Abby may have transitioned to the world of the wealthy with seemingly little issue, but Lil didn't know where to begin to prepare it. "Will you come with me? I can't go there alone."

Her friend looked dubious and said, "You know Abby isn't wild about me."

Lil reached for Alethea's hand and gave it a reassuring squeeze. "I'll talk to her. I'm sure she'll add you to the list if I ask."

Alethea returned the squeeze absently, her growing excitement with some idea quickly overshadowed her concern. "Big party at Dominic Corisi's place?"

"No at his . . ."

A huge smile spread across Alethea's face. "Sounds like something that would have the very best security."

Oh, I shouldn't have said anything. "No, Al. Can't you just be there for me like a normal friend? Just this once?"

"I'll be there," Alethea promised in a tone that did not make Lil feel any better.

"I mean it." Lil looked her friend right in the eye, hoping her friend would heed her advice this one time. "Don't try to circumvent his security. He takes his privacy really seriously. You could get hurt."

Alethea straightened proudly, tossing her head in a way that reminded Lil of a wild horse. "Or I could get in and imagine the contracts I would pull in after that."

Lil groaned. "I'm imagining many possible outcomes and none of them good."

"I'll keep you on speed dial, okay?" Alethea mimed dialing her number. "First sign of trouble I'll pretend I'm lost and I'll call you. Does that make you feel better?"

"Not really." Lil sighed. "You're crazy, you know that?"

"Lucky for me, that was a mutual prerequisite to this friendship."

"Think you're so funny, huh?" Lil pulled her friend close for a one-arm hug.

Alethea returned the hug and gave Colby a quick kiss on the cheek. "See you in New York, Lil."

Conceding to the fact that nothing was likely to stop her friend at this point, Lil said, "It's at Dominic's . . ."

Alethea interrupted Lil before she let herself out of the penthouse. "Don't tell me. You know it's more fun for me to figure it out myself. Oh, and call your damn sister."

A FEW MINUTES past eight that night, there was another knock at the door. Lil looked down at her black cotton T-shirt and matching sweat shorts. She wasn't dressed for company, she was dressed for settling down with the bowl of popcorn she'd just made and watching the sappy movie she'd planned to escape into.

Why does this place even have an intercom if no one is going to use it? Lil swung the door open.

Jake.

Beautiful, perfectly groomed Jake. The man had probably been born in a charcoal suit. Lil's hand went to the back of her neck instinctively pushing at the curls she knew had already broken free of the loose knot she'd tied them back in.

He looked as irritated as he sounded. "I could be anybody. No security system is going to keep you safe if you open the door for anyone who knocks."

She was tempted to tell him how his "security" had already failed once that day, but she held her tongue. She didn't bother to curb her sarcasm. "Hi, Jake. It's nice to see you, too. I thought you went back to New York."

He scowled. "I did."

"Did you forget something here?" she asked sweetly. Was it wrong to hope the man wasn't perfect?

He shook his head and walked toward her with purpose. The hair on the back of Lil's neck tingled and she bit her lip. There was something different about him tonight. Something both dangerous and incredibly hot at the same time.

She took a step back.

"Where is Colby?" he asked softly, prowling toward her.

"In bed for the night," Lil said hoarsely. *Exactly where I should be*, she thought. *Alone*, she added for the benefit of her raging libido.

He advanced until they were so close that she could see the desire burning in his eyes. "I have responsibilities in New York. Meetings scheduled. Documents to prepare before the weekend. I don't have time for this," he said gruffly.

Lil swallowed nervously, feeling desire whip through her in response. Was he saying what she thought he was saying?

"But I'm here." He reached out and cupped the back of her head, pulling her closer, tilting her head up to his.

Lil licked her lips. *Yes, you are.*

"I can't concentrate in New York. All I can think about is this . . ." His head swooped down and he claimed her. His tongue slipped inside her lips and drew an instant and overwhelming response from every inch of Lil. He was savoring, devouring her and she couldn't get enough of it.

She welcomed him passionately. Her hands slid beneath his jacket and gripped the rippling muscles of his back. He put a hand on her behind and pulled her against him, positioning her against his excitement. "And this."

Oh God, me too. Lil sucked in a breath as her body clenched and moistened. Still, she reached for some sanity. "Didn't we agree that this was a mistake?"

He explored her neck with his lips, teasing just below her ear with the tip of this tongue. His hot breath added to her building excitement as she remembered how it had warmed her thighs and other areas of her body that were already pulsing and begging for his attention.

"You can send me away." His strong hands negated his words, holding her, seeking out the entry beneath her clothing. "Say the word and I'll go."

I should.

Nothing about this made any sense.

He'd made no promises to her, but oddly that was what she found tempting. She wouldn't have believed declarations of devotion. This was real. This was what men wanted and, at that moment, she couldn't deny that it was what she wanted, too. She wanted to lose herself in the overwhelming sensations his nearness elicited, drown in the escape that this level of passion offered.

One of his hands slid beneath the back elastic of her shorts. "Look at me," he commanded.

Lil had a flash of their first time together. Wonderful as it had been, he had given very little of himself, revealed even less. This time she wanted more. She would demand more.

"I have one condition to us doing this," she said breathlessly and fingered the buttons on his shirt.

"Name it," he growled.

"I want to play a game this time," she said and peered up at him from beneath her lashes.

"A game?" His head pulled back. "I don't do anything that involves restraint or pain."

She slapped his chest playfully. "And you think I do?"

He leaned down to nuzzle her neck. "I have no idea." His hand slid beneath her waistband again, this time also sliding beneath the back of her silk panties and closing on her hind cheek with a proprietorial squeeze. "But I want to know. I want to know everything about you."

She smiled. "Perfect, then you'll enjoy this game." She stepped back and away from him. "Have you ever played truth or dare?"

"No," he said and his frustration with her insertion of dialogue into what was a highly charged sexual moment was clear in both his facial expression and tone.

"Well, this is a variation of it. Truth or strip. I'll ask you a question and if you don't feel comfortable answering it, you remove an article of clothing."

He reached for her again, but she moved out of his reach.

"An article of your clothing," she clarified.

"Wouldn't it be nicer to simply let me explore you? I missed a few places last time and I'd like to rectify that."

Tempting as that offer was, she moved even further away and shook her head. "I'll start with an easy one. Do you have a middle name?"

"No," he said and advanced toward her.

She skirted around the couch and, with the furniture safely between them, instructed, "Now it's your turn. Ask me something."

"Do you always have to make things more difficult than they have to be?" he said and took a step around the couch.

She retreated in the opposite direction. "A nice question, one that would help you know me better."

He advanced again and said in a honey tone, "I am trying to know you better."

This time she stood her ground, refusing to budge.

He held his distance although the heat in his eyes suggested that their game was exciting him. Forcing him to play by her rules was an incredible aphrodisiac—for both of them. He growled, "Did you pass your exam?"

"I think so," she answered happily, loving how close he looked to ending this and taking her right there on the floor. Lil's thighs quivered at the thought, anticipating wrapping around him and welcoming him into her.

When none of her clothing was removed, he said, "Let's skip the game."

"It gets better," she assured him and knew that it would. Their first time had been incredible, and Lil was already wet and ready for him even though they had barely touched. Can you improve on incredible? She was more than a little willing to find out. "I wanted to give you an example. Now we can have a little fun. How old were you when you first had sex?"

"Seventeen," he answered, looking slightly more interested in the game. "And you?"

"Twenty-one," she said. *Seventeen, huh?* She'd have to ask for those details at another time. She didn't want another woman in this moment. "How many partners have you had?"

He shrugged his jacket off.

"How about you?" he asked.

"One," she said then quickly corrected herself, "well, two if I count you."

He didn't like that comment very much, nor did he like that no clothing had been lost in the exchange. "Count me," he growled.

Lil smiled. Ouch, was his ego that sensitive? "Do you have any brothers or sisters?" she asked.

"No," he answered. "Do you pleasure yourself?"

"Of course," she answered easily. "Do you?"

He removed his tie and was looking less pleased as the game continued. "This game isn't fair. You'll say anything."

Let him stew a bit. Lil challenged, "That's where you're wrong. To know what I won't say, you'll have to get to know me better, won't you?"

An odd expression flitted across his face, as if he'd realized that the game was so much more than a stalling tactic. Tonight he was going to have to earn the pleasure. She figured a man like him would love a good puzzle and she was right. He considered the situation for a moment and then inspiration curled his lips into a smile. "Were you thinking of me when you did it the last time?"

She slipped her shirt up over her head and dropped it on the floor behind her.

His smile widened.

"Are you dating anyone?" she asked.

"No," he said simply and she believed him. "Are you?"

"No," she said. Now onto something she'd been asking herself for weeks. "Why did you go bowling with me that first night?"

He looked like he was debating sharing or stripping, then he said, "You were the most beautiful woman I'd ever seen."

She cocked a skeptical eyebrow. "You know this is a truth game, right?"

He stepped closer and caressed her cheek with one gentle hand. "I have no reason to lie." He traced the edge of her cheek with his thumb, softly explored the curve of her lips and asked huskily, "Did I really misunderstand your intention on the island? Were you offering yourself to me?"

Lil slid her shorts down so she could step out of them, tossing them behind her. He explored her newly exposed hips. "Where do your parents live?" she asked.

His hand stilled. "I don't discuss my parents." His reaction was so strong that it broke the mood for a moment.

Another question best discussed some other time. Lil decided to lighten the mood. "Your shirt then."

His smile returned. He slowly unbuttoned it and tossed it behind him. "What are you most afraid of?"

Lil unsnapped her bra and let it drop to the floor. She heard the hiss of his quickly indrawn breath and reveled in being able to drive him to the edge.

"Have you ever been in love?" she asked, taking advantage of their intimacy.

"No," he said, settling his hand on one of her breasts, rubbing his thumb across one of her already erect nipples. "Have you?"

His rhythmic circling made it suddenly difficult for her to focus on what he was asking. Her other breast tightened and yearned. She fought for control. "I thought I was once, but I was wrong."

His hand stilled. "Colby's father?"

She smiled sadly. "It's my turn to ask a question."

He leaned down and took her other eager breast into his mouth, circling it with his tongue in much the same way this thumb had teased her other. She gasped at his gentle nip and threw her head back with pleasure when the circling continued, in union, pausing periodically to rub or lick the tip. His mouth found its way to her collarbone and back up to her ear where he whispered, "He was a fool."

She closed her eyes. "I was the fool."

He pulled her full against him, wrapping both of his arms around her waist, settling bare chest against bare chest and waited until she dared to peer up at him again before he spoke. "No, you charge full ahead and you hold nothing back—but that doesn't make you a fool."

How had tenderness wormed its way into their exchange? Lil didn't want this to matter because she didn't want to care when he walked away. Still, she couldn't help but ask, "Have you ever done that? Just jumped in . . . even when you knew you shouldn't . . . because you couldn't help yourself?"

"Yes," he said, his eyes burned down into hers. "With you." He kissed her lips lightly. "You drive me crazy, but I can't stay away from you."

"Take off your pants," Lil commanded.

"That's not a question."

"It's not an option either."

He chuckled and bent to kiss her again, but she turned her head away. When he lifted his head in confusion she ran a hand over the stubble that was just beginning to show through on his otherwise perfectly smooth face.

She said, "Your pants."

An excited flush spread up his neck and across his face. He removed the rest of his clothing with remarkable speed and returned to his initial position, this time he freed his erection and pressing against her. He bent to remove her panties, trailing kisses down her stomach as he did.

Once she was completely unclothed, he knelt before her and held her still with a strong hand on either hip. His hands sought and worshipped every inch of her.

With a strong move, he lifted one of her legs and hooked it over his shoulder, opening her wide before him, an opportunity he took full advantage of with his mouth. Lil clutched at the back of his head when his tongue tasted and invaded. Each flick was strategic and sent her head sagging backward in ecstasy.

He stood and their kiss tasted of her own excitement, something that drove her over the edge and she gladly sank to her knees before him, returning the favor. Feeling him swell and jut against her suckling increased her already mind-blowing fervor. She cupped him from below and rubbed the area at his base with her thumb, reveling at the moan that escaped him. The muscles of his thighs tensed beneath one of her hands. When she thought he could take no more, she stopped and moved her kisses to his stomach.

"You're killing me," he groaned.

"What do you want, Jake?" she asked, knowing the answer but needing to hear him say it.

He hauled her up to her feet and said, "I want to take you now, make you mine."

She looked into his golden-brown eyes and said, "Do it. Let go and just do it."

He lifted her, repositioned her so that her legs wrapped around his waist, and entered her with one powerful thrust. She threw her head back with a cry of pleasure. He took two steps toward the wall and held her there, off the floor, as he pounded again and again, deeper and deeper.

A wave of warmth spread from deep inside of Lil and tingled outward through her, increasing and pulsing through her with each thrust. This was a taking that surpassed any she'd dreamt possible. There was no him, no her . . . only them and a wild feeling of freedom.

He came with a shudder as her own release had begun to ebb.

"Did you?" he asked and she bit her lip. Was silence a lie if it brought them both further pleasure?

He kissed her deeply and stayed within her.

Without hearing his request, she knew what he wanted. She tightened and released her inner muscles on him, finding a comfortable rhythm that not only brought him back to life within her, but also stimulated her in a new and wondrous way.

He slid himself out of her, picked her up and carried her to one side of the couch. He turned her and bent her over the large, cushioned arm of it. Lil looked over her shoulder at him and shuddered as his hands closed over her hips, holding her still while his ever-hardening shaft teased her outer folds. He kissed the back of her neck, trailed kisses down her spine, his hot breath tickling as it excited. When he reached the curve of her buttocks with his lips, he straightened and placed a foot between hers and moved them apart impatiently.

He slipped a finger inside her and continued to kiss the back of her legs, the curve of her cheeks. In and out he pumped until she was clutching onto the couch with both hands and was oh so ready for him. He straightened and she felt him, fully erect again, graze her leg.

Then he was inside her again, one hand on either hip, moving her to meet him, building a rhythm between them that she could not and had no desire to fight. Their first coupling had been amazing, but he lasted even longer this time and her final orgasm was even more intense and devastating as it shook her. She came with a profane exclamation she could not contain and he joined her with one last deep thrust.

Withdrawing, he turned her to him, lifted her again, and sank onto the couch with her sideways on his lap.

"I'll never look at this couch the same way again," she joked into his bare chest.

"Ssssh," he said, but he smiled.

In union, their breathing slowly returned to normal.

A thought came to him that tensed him slightly beneath her in an entirely different way than earlier. "I didn't use a condom." He groaned.

"Shit," Lil said, sitting straight up in his lap. "You're right."

He rubbed a hand across his eyes as if trying to wipe away his confusion. "I've never forgotten before."

She had, but that was why she'd gone an additional step. "Don't worry, I'm on the pill."

"It's about more than that." He absently played with the hair that spilled down her back.

"Do you have a disease I should know about?" she joked.

He shook his head and pulled her against his chest. "No, but not using one was completely irresponsible and I . . ."

This time she was the one who tensed. He was probably more worried about what he could catch from her than the reverse. "And you're always responsible. Unlike me. I know. I get it."

He soothed her like one would a child, running his hand through her hair gently and then cupped her chin. "I'm not judging you. I'm just questioning my own sanity."

That didn't make her feel much better.

"I'm not sure either option is very flattering." She struggled to free herself from him, but he held her on his lap.

"What if something comes from today?" he asked in his oh-so-obnoxiously-rational tone.

Lil broke free of his hold and stood. "You mean, what if I get pregnant? Wow, you know how to kill a mood."

What had felt so right a moment ago now made Lil feel vulnerable and defensive. She was in the process of putting her shirt back on when he stopped her by standing in front of her and taking both of her shoulders into his hands. "I'm serious."

She lashed out. "So am I. If anything comes from today, it'll be my concern, not yours."

"What is that supposed to mean?"

Fear surfaced as anger. "We are not even dating. We're just fucking."

His face darkened. "You make it sound cheap."

She struggled to get away, but he held her there, intent on making his message heard. "I would never leave you with a baby . . . . *my* baby."

"There is zero possibility that I would terminate a pregnancy."

His hands gripped her shoulders tighter. "I know that. I would take care of you. You'd live with me."

"Are you serious?" she joked. Jake's steady gaze held hers. "Oh, my God, you're serious." Her heart pounded in her chest. "I'm not pregnant so we don't have to have this conversation."

"You could be and we do."

Lil shook her head vehemently. "Even if you have super sperm and I'm already pregnant, there is no way I would move in with you like that."

His hands loosened and massaged her shoulders gently. "You're right. We'd have to get married."

Lil cut in, "Stop. Stop right there. Let's not go nuts. I'm

not pregnant. We're not getting married. This whole thing between us is just a . . ."

"Don't say it," he said, his hands stilling.

She stopped.

She met his eyes and then looked away, unable to decipher the emotions she saw churning there. "What happens if you don't say it?" he asked softly.

She studied his broad, lightly haired chest.

"What happens if I don't either?" he continued. "What if we just see where this goes?" He rubbed a thumb down her jaw pensively as if he were trying to solve an equation.

Her throat dried, making her first attempt at a rebuttal impossible.

"Let me stay tonight," he suggested and Lil panicked.

Staying would lead to wanting to believe. Believing would only lead to heartache. Why prolong the process? Lil finished putting her shirt on and hastily slid back into her underwear. Jake was dangerous because he threatened the sensible path she'd chosen for herself. Why couldn't she have met him back when she'd proudly thrown caution to the wind?

The universe had a cruel sense of humor.

"There is only one bedroom set up and the crib is in there," she said and tossed his underwear and pants to him. "You can't stay."

"Come with me to New York," he said as he stepped back into both, never taking his eyes off of her. "Not tonight, tomorrow. You and Colby can stay with me at my place until we figure this out."

Tempting as it was, that wasn't a life that Lil wanted for herself and her child. "I can't do that, Jake. I know it doesn't look like I am—but I'm really trying to make better decisions. For me, for Colby, for our future. Moving in with you is not a good decision."

He bent to pick his rumpled dress shirt off the floor, donned it and began to button it absently. "I can take care of you—both of you. You'll never want for anything."

He offered so much and so little at the same time.

"You don't understand yet, Jake. What I want can't be bought for me. I want to look at myself in the mirror and respect who I see. I want to be a strong, independent woman so that Colby will grow up knowing what really matters in life." She turned away from him. "And so far I'm not doing very well. What kind of example am I for Colby? I barely know you and look at us."

He went to stand behind her. Touching her lower back with one warm hand. "Whatever is between us, Lil, it doesn't change that you are a wonderful mother."

Don't be nice, Jake. I don't want to like you.

"I wish I could believe that," Lil mumbled.

Jake wrapped his arms around her waist and pulled her gently back against him, talking softly into her ear. "I envy your daughter. She has a mother who loves her fiercely and unconditionally. That's the gift you will give her. Wanting me doesn't make you weak or dependent. And I'm not a little boy, Lil. You can't drive me away with your sarcasm or change my mind about what I want. I don't know what we have and I don't know if it will last, but it's not cheap, Lil."

She looked back at him. "Then what is it?"

He was quiet for a moment, then said, "Do we need to label it for you to be comfortable with it? Call me a boyfriend. Call me a lover. I don't care."

Lil turned away again, removed his hands from her stomach and stepped out of his embrace. "I care. And I'm not looking for an empty label, either."

He took one of her arms in his hand and turned her to face him. "What do you want, Lil?"

She shook her head and refused to look up at him. *I want the stupid fairy tale*, but who could admit that? She wanted to be loved, needed, cherished—all the cornball stuff she vehemently denied. The best response she could give him was the truth. "More than this."

"Do you want me to lie? Say something we both don't mean yet?" His hand tightened on her arm.

Lil pulled her arm free. "Been there, done that."

She stepped away, but he followed her, putting a hand beneath her chin and forcing her to meet his eyes. "I'm not your ex, Lil."

Feeling cornered, she snapped, "No, you're not. You're not even my present. We're nothing to each other except a bad decision. I'd like you to go now."

"Lil—"

Like removing a Band-Aid, Lil wanted the pain to come in one swift rip at a time of her choosing. She pushed against him with her words. "I mean it, Jake. We're not good for each other. We're too different. This . . . this attraction between us is something that is better just denied."

"That's what you really want?" He sounded almost sad.

"Yes, that's what I want."

"I'm not sorry I came back up here."

Don't be so damned sweet, Jake! It would be too easy to accept what little he was offering her and confuse his kindness with what she really craved from him. "I'm not either, but from now on we have to keep a distance from each other."

He looked down at her like he wanted to kiss her again, but instead, he said, "This isn't over."

A question leapt out of her, as unplanned as it was quickly regretted. "Will you be at Abby and Dominic's party this weekend?"

"Yes," he said simply.

She bit her bottom lip to stop herself from saying more. She didn't want to be happy to hear that they would see each other again.

I'm such an idiot.

She walked to the door and opened it.

He followed her, but stopped in front of her. He leaned in and gave her a deep kiss, the kind that made her want to retract everything she'd just said and find a babysitter for the night. She sagged against him.

He put her back gently. "I'll see you at the party."

"Yes," she croaked.

"Call me if you change your mind," he said and she hated that she wasn't able to hide her surge of attraction from him.

"I won't," she said with determination.

After one final, light kiss to her cheek, he smiled, walked through the door and said, "You might."

She closed the door behind him and stood there for a moment, just holding the handle to steady herself.

I can't.

Chapter Nine

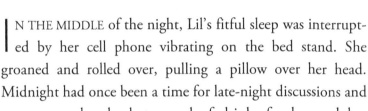

IN THE MIDDLE of the night, Lil's fitful sleep was interrupted by her cell phone vibrating on the bed stand. She groaned and rolled over, pulling a pillow over her head. Midnight had once been a time for late-night discussions and a cue to order the last round of drinks for her and her friends, but motherhood had a way of changing a person's inner clock. Five of midnight might as well be called five of *this-had-better-be-important-because-if-Colby-wakes-up-I'm-going-to-kill-you.*

Her phone vibrated again, Lil pushed back the comforter, grabbed her phone and padded to the living room to answer it. Alethea's name showed on the caller ID. She wouldn't call at this hour unless it was important.

Lil plopped onto the couch. "What do you need?"

"Did I wake you? Sorry, but this can't wait," Alethea said. "We have a problem. I've been looking into this party you say your sister has planned for Saturday and something isn't right about it."

Rubbing a tired hand over her still half-closed eyes, Lil asked, "What are you talking about?"

Alethea continued on at what felt like breakneck speed to Lil. "There is a buzz in the hacker community that something big is going down and the party is a cover."

Lil turned onto her side on the couch with a yawn, her eyes closing even as she spoke. "You always think something suspicious is going on."

"I'm usually right," her friend said impatiently. "I know your sister is in love, but you two don't really know who you are dealing with. Dominic didn't make his fortune by playing nice and Jake hasn't been crisscrossing the country for the past week looking for the perfect engagement present. Everything leads back to that party and anyone he has spoken to has received some form of hush money. Not enough, is my guess, since there is chatter."

"Maybe they are planning a surprise for Abby," Lil mumbled.

"Or maybe your sister is in danger."

That woke Lil up. Her eyes flew open and she sat straight up.

Alethea continued, "What if Dominic is using your sister as a cover for something he doesn't want people to know about? Their whole engagement could be a sham. And worse, what if your sister stumbles onto what is going on? She'd be a danger to them."

Hugging her knees to her on the couch, Lil said, "That's a lot of ifs. Do you have any proof?"

"Jeremy does."

"Jeremy Kater? I haven't heard from him in years."

"No one has. I don't think he leaves his basement. He

doesn't see anyone, either. It's really a bit creepy."

"But he saw you?"

"He used to have a crush on me. We've kept in touch. Remember how he used to play video games for ten hours a day back in school? He's taken it to a whole new level. It's an obsession now. But he is the best hacker I know. It's how he gets all the games before they come out. Sometimes I slide him a little cash to get the plans for a building or to check out something for me. He prefers to stay below the radar, though, so I had to promise him more than money to get him to hack other hackers."

Lil shuddered. "You didn't . . ."

Her friend laughed. "No, get your mind out of the gutter. I promised him that I'd help him find a date."

"That's it?"

"Oh, you haven't seen him recently. It's not going to be easy. Anyway, Dominic and Jake are definitely hiding something. You should warn your sister."

"And say what? That you have a bad feeling about the party?" Lil's stomach clenched and churned. *That would go over well.* "She's going to think that I'm stirring up trouble."

"Well you can't say nothing."

"We have no proof. You could be wrong." Lil stood and began to pace nervously. "I can't get involved in this."

"Ooooo-kay."

Lil's back stiffened at her friend's tone. "Don't say it like that."

"Like what?"

"Like you're disappointed in me. Do you know how bad

this could go if you're wrong? I can't do this."

"When did you become so terrified of being wrong?"

When I realized that my actions don't only affect me and my future. "Considering the consequences of your actions does not make you a coward. If we had proof, nothing could stop me from telling Abby. But, Al, we don't know any of this for sure. I'm not going to Abby without something definite. Can Jeremy get that?"

"He might be able to remote access Jake's personal computer and see if he left an email trail. Maybe he got sloppy and mentioned what the payoffs were about."

"That sounds illegal," Lil said.

Alethea's tone turned droll. "Well, you could always go up to Jake and ask him if he and Dominic are using your sister and if they intend to dispose of her when they're done."

"Now you're just trying to scare me." Lil shuddered.

Alethea sighed impatiently. "No, I'm trying to get you to see how serious this could be. We need to know what Dominic is hiding and the only way to do that is to find out what he has Jake looking for."

"And we can do that without Jake knowing we did it?"

"Jeremy is good. He can get in and out without being detected."

Oh, God. Oh, God. Oh, God.

This was exactly the kind of thing Lil had told herself she would never do again. But what if Abby really was in danger? She'd never forgive herself if she could have prevented it but had let her fear stop her from getting involved. "Okay, do it."

Instantly, Alethea was all business. "Is Jake still up in the Boston area? We need to find a way to keep him off his computer for a few hours."

"I have no idea where he is," Lil said definitively and perhaps too quickly.

"So you haven't heard from him at all?" Alethea asked slowly with growing suspicion. It's not easy to get anything by a best friend.

Lil covered her face with a hand and reluctantly admitted, "He was here earlier tonight."

Sounding disgustingly happy about being right again, Alethea said, "Oh, he has it bad. This will be a breeze. Call him up first thing in the morning and make a date for Thursday."

Lil shook her head at her friend even though she knew she couldn't see her. "I can't. I told him it's over."

"Well, tell him you changed your mind."

A wave of emotion washed over Lil. "It's not that simple." *I told myself it was over, too.*

"Do you want to know if your sister is safe or not?"

"I do."

"Then call Jake. Take him somewhere public if you're that worried about sleeping with him again."

She was more worried about getting her heart broken. "Fine. I'll call him, but he might already be back in New York."

Alethea chuckled. "I highly doubt that."

"Good night."

"Text me when you have a set time."

"Be careful, Al."

"Always, Lil. Always."

MID-MORNING, LIL HUNG up at the first ring of Jake's phone as she continued to debate her present course of action. None of this was a good idea. Hacking someone's computer was definitely illegal, probably prison kind of illegal.

Dominic and Jake might not be breaking any laws and that would make the only criminals in the scenario—her and her friends.

Or Alethea was right and Abby had gotten mixed up in something dangerous.

Please, universe, please don't let me be wrong here.

Or, if I'm wrong, please don't let it screw everything up for Abby.

Just this once, give me an outcome I don't regret.

She dialed Jake's cell again.

"Lil?" Jake asked, sounding a mixture of surprised and concerned.

"Hi, Jake." *Don't overthink this, just jump.* "I was wondering if you were still in Boston."

She heard him catch his breath.

"I'm still here."

Just do it. Just ask. "Would you want to spend an hour . . . three hours tops . . . " Oh, hell, how long did it take to hack into someone's computer? "Maybe the whole morning with me and Colby tomorrow? If you're not busy. I mean, I know you're busy, but it doesn't have to be the whole day. Maybe we could go to breakfast or lunch or something . . ." She tapered off lamely. "I think we should make it a public place, though." When he didn't say anything at first she added, "Could we try to be . . . friends?" She groaned inwardly.

"How does nine sound?"

She swallowed hard. "That would be fine."

"I'll pick you up."

Well, this couldn't possibly be more awkward.

"Great. See you tomorrow, Jake."

He said, "Lil?" with a hint of anticipation that made her clench her phone.

"Yes?"

"I'm glad you called."

Suddenly feeling shaky, she sank into one of the thickly cushioned chairs in her living room. *You wouldn't be if you knew why.* "Me, too," she said softly and hung up before she said anything stupid. *God, help me. Me, too.*

JAKE HUNG UP the phone and smiled.

She wants to see me.

Common sense should have told him that his best course would be to return to New York now, but common sense had pretty much deserted him days ago.

He wanted to prove something tomorrow—prove it to Lil as well as to himself. What they had didn't have to be cheap. He was drawn to her on more than one level. No, he wasn't looking to marry her, but that didn't mean that his only interest in her was sexual.

He called Marie.

"Marie, I'm still in Boston."

"Good."

"I need your advice on something."

"With Lil?"

There was no reason to hide anything from Marie. Where he was concerned, she had an uncanny ability to know how he felt about something before he did. She called it a mother's intuition; something he'd always scoffed at since she didn't have children and she certainly wasn't his mother.

He spoke to his actual mother as little as possible. Neither of his parents were particularly affectionate people. Bi-annual phone conversations provided ample contact in his opinion and he was pretty sure they were in complete agreement.

He couldn't imagine Lil ever having that relationship with Colby. The mere idea of it made him smile. In-law apartments were created for mothers like Lil. She'd want to be right there for all of Colby's life milestones.

"Marie, I'm taking Lil and Colby out for the day tomorrow." He hesitated to label it and then found that he wanted to. "It's our first date."

He could feel Marie's approval through the phone. "Oh, Jake, I'm so glad."

He took women out to dinner and to events, usually to showcase them or because a certain event required a couple. It was enough for most women to simply be seen with him, but this was different. He wanted this to be special, a day she would always remember. "Where do you think they would want to go?"

"Didn't you go to school in Cambridge?"

"Yes."

"Why don't you take her somewhere you've spent some time? It's a nice way to let her get to know you better."

He doubted she wanted to visit the Financial District or the bowels of a library. Outside of work, he couldn't think of any place that had any significance to him.

That realization struck him as a bit sad. A month ago he'd thought he had everything, now he was beginning to wonder if he had anything at all.

"Lil isn't like the women I'm used to dating."

"Thank God," Marie said and chuckled. "Did I say that out loud?"

"You did."

She was unrepentant as usual. "I don't know what Lil likes, Jake, so I can't tell you where to take her. Trust your instincts. You know what she cares about. Start there."

"What would I do without you, Marie?"

"I ask myself that every day," she teased gently. "Now, go and plan your date. Show that girl the man I know you are."

"Marie, I . . ." he started to say something then stopped.

"I know," she replied, understanding more than he did what he had difficulty saying. "Don't forget to tell me how it went."

"I won't," he answered automatically and hung up.

He smiled.

Marie was a genius.

There were two things Jake knew that Lil loved, but the question was if he could combine them. He used the search engine on his phone and reached for a notepad as he began to find exactly what he was looking for.

Who knew that planning a date could actually be *fun*?

Chapter Ten

THE NEXT MORNING, even as she readied herself and Colby, Lil wavered. She really should call a halt to this whole insanity. Maybe she should just tell Abby everything and let her decide how to move forward with it.

No, putting the weight of this problem on her sister would be the coward's way out. Why ruin her happiness if there was a chance that this was all a paranoid conspiracy theory hatched up by Alethea?

Alethea. The mere mention of her friend's name would be enough for Abby to dismiss any allegations unless there was hard proof of wrongdoing.

Abby had never made a secret that she disapproved of her best friend. She didn't like that Alethea had been booted out of every private school before her parents had sent her to public school as a punishment—a punishment Alethea had embraced.

Born to an upper-class family, Alethea had no fear of authority and she had the resources to defy them. Abby had spent many nights attempting to explain the danger in the differences between their situations to Lil, but Lil had refused to listen to her. Yes, Alethea broke the rules sometimes merely for the rush of doing it and some of her ideas had landed Lil in some sticky situations but a friend isn't someone who never makes mistakes. A friend is someone who loves you right through the ones you make yourself.

And Alethea always had.

It had been Alethea she'd called the night Dirk had walked away from her, Alethea who had convinced her to eat if only for the sake of the baby growing within her and had bolstered her confidence enough to tell Abby she was pregnant.

Looking back now, Abby hadn't said anything wrong when she finally had told her; she just hadn't said what Lil had yearned to hear—that she loved her and that they would get through it together. No, instead, she had talked about getting health insurance, finding a good doctor, and starting prenatal care immediately.

All very good advice.

And maybe the only way Abby knew how to deal with the unexpected. She'd had to be strong for so long, maybe she'd forgotten how to share a moment of weakness.

It hadn't been with malice that Lil had chosen Alethea to bring to her first ultrasound and to invite to be her Lamaze partner. As much as she'd known that Abby had been hurt by the decision, it had also been Alethea she'd chosen to be with her in the delivery room. Things had become so bad between her and Abby by then that they'd barely been speaking; neither knowing quite how to remedy the situation or if it was even worth trying to.

Lil had considered explaining her choices to Abby, but none of her explanations would have improved the situation. The simple fact was that birthing someone had been full-on scary to Lil and she'd wanted someone at her side who could overlook any weakness she might reveal in the process.

So, Colby had been held first by a friend and then by her aunt; something Abby hadn't yet forgiven Alethea for, not even as her happiness with Dominic had spilled outward and given them a second chance at sisterhood.

With motherhood had come the humility to recognize that Abby was not the only flawed member of their tiny family. Abby had always been there for her even if it hadn't been the way Lil would have liked, but Lil hadn't returned the favor. Beneath her tough exterior, Lil acknowledged that insecurities had driven some of her—oh, hell, many of her actions.

But wasn't that what a new day provided?

A chance to begin again?

She was going to become the sister she should have always been. This time she was going to rescue Abby.

Chapter Eleven

JAKE WALTON IN a suit was sexy enough, but the man who had shown up in khaki shorts and a blue polo shirt took Lil's breath away. His shorts stopped mid-thigh, long enough to be fashionable, but short enough to remind Lil of what he had looked like with much less on.

Lil looked away.

Better decisions could only come from gaining some control over her libido. Seriously, Jake was just another man. An incredibly gorgeous, sexually talented, inspiration-for-dreams-you-don't-want-to-wake-up-from man, but that didn't mean she couldn't keep a clear head today.

Lil snuck another quick perusal.

Damn.

Dressed in a simple brown cotton skirt, light green blouse and sandals, Lil was determined that their day together would stay as tame as the clothing she'd chosen. She bent to place her daughter in the car seat. "Come on in," she said as she collected the necessary supplies for the day. "We're ready."

Colby babbled happily as she was secured into her seat.

Lil swung her diaper bag up onto her shoulder, reaching down to pick up the car seat.

Jake's hand beat her to it. "I'll carry her; I bet she's getting heavy."

He smiled down at Colby who smiled back at him and Lil fought the desire to rip her child out of his hands and run. Neither of them had any business getting attached to Jake. Today was not about that. Tomorrow, things would go right back to being over.

Lil took a deep breath and reminded herself that this was for Abby.

"Thank you," she said and hoped she didn't sound as stressed as she felt. He was going to get suspicious if she looked like a trapped animal the whole day. *Be cool. Be casual.* "I couldn't find my stroller, so hopefully there is one wherever we're going."

"I had yours stored in your trunk."

"Of course." Lil smoothed her nervous hands on her skirt and picked up her purse. "Then let's go."

At least having Colby with them insured that nothing would happen between them.

Bringing her had been a good idea.

Unless Jake really is dangerous and now I put my daughter in jeopardy, too. Oh, shit.

You're losing it, Lil.

Jake had never given her a reason to think that he would ever hurt her or her child. She was letting Alethea's paranoia make her nuts.

The trip down the elevator was painfully silent as was the

wait for the car to be brought out of the parking lot. Jake opened the door for Lil and handed her the car seat, watching as she secured it.

Not the mannerisms of a madman.

Relax.

Lil jumped when Jake asked, "Do you want me to drive?"

Since her legs were ready to betray her by shaking, Lil nodded. Driving while deceiving was never a safe option. *Officer, I'm sorry I didn't see that red light I was too busy thinking about what Jake was going to say if he ever discovered why I asked him to come out with me today.*

She gladly handed Jake her keys.

Buckled into the passenger seat, Lil faced forward, but watched Jake out of the corner of her eye. He'd secured his own seat belt, but hadn't started the car.

"We can't be friends, Lil," he announced to the steering wheel.

"Excuse me?" Lil swallowed nervously. *In the movies, this is where he would tell me that I should have minded my own business—that he had hoped things would go differently, but I knew too much to be allowed to live.*

Jake looked across at her, the intensity in his eyes trapping her like a deer in headlights.

"I don't think I have to tell you why it's not possible."

Because friends don't bury friends in shallow graves in the woods?

Lil bit back a nervous giggle.

He said, "I've been thinking about how you called what

we're doing cheap. It doesn't have to be. I do care about you, Lil, and I'd like for us to start over."

No, no, no. Do not even go there. I like being afraid of you better than this. This path only leads to a tsunami of guilt. "Jake, please . . ."

He turned in his seat and took her hand. "Hear me out. You took me by surprise and I handled the situation poorly. Everything you said the other day was spot-on right. We don't know each other, but we can change that. I'm not here because Dominic sent me. Today, I'm here because I want to be. I want to give us a chance—not as friends, but as whatever this is—wherever this goes. This is a date, Lil; make no mistake about that. Our first date, one of many to come, and hopefully one that you'll never forget."

I can pretty much guarantee that I'll remember today.

He was waiting for her to say something.

She removed her hand from his. *I am going to hell for this. Yep, forget about prison, this is the fiery after-life kind of wrong.* "I can't promise you anything, Jake."

His eyes smoldered with emotion as if her words only made him want her more. "You don't have to."

Lil turned forward in her seat and clasped her hands in her lap, trying to keep her tone as cheerful as possible. "So, where are we going?"

"I thought I'd surprise you."

Oh, you did.

Trust me, you did.

"WHAT ARE WE doing here?" Lil asked as they parked her car

in front of the Boston Museum's School of Fine Arts.

Jake walked around the car to open the door for her before he answered. "On Thursday mornings the school has an art program for the very young and their mothers. They make their own paints and sometimes display their creations in the atrium. They have graciously allowed us to join the class today."

Once Colby was settled into her stroller, Jake tipped a young man who had apparently been hired to park the car for them. As they walked into the building together, Lil asked, "You really signed us up for an art class?"

"Unless you'd rather do something else?"

"No, this is fine."

This is perfect, actually. Well, it would be perfect if I weren't a complete ass.

Lil followed Jake through the halls to a small classroom where four mothers and their babies were gathered around one large round table. The children ranged in age from near Colby's age to one that looked like she was almost two.

A casually dressed, gray-haired woman in a large clear plastic apron met them as they entered the door. Her face looked years younger than her hair implied. "You must be Miss Dartley." She shook Lil's hand. "And is this Colby?" She leaned down to smile at the child and then greeted Jake. "Mr. Walton, it is an honor to have you join us today. Your donation was more than generous and will allow us to expand this program."

Jake accepted her gratitude with a nod and a smile.

The woman turned to the mothers behind her. "Ladies,

today's class is going to be a bit different. We have some special guests today. This is Mr. Walton, a long-time supporter of the arts in Boston and his . . ." She turned to Lil as she stumbled for how to describe her.

"Just call me Lil," Lil supplied hastily.

"Welcome, Lil," two of the mothers said almost in union. The others simply waved.

The older woman continued, "Mr. Walton flew in a surprise that I hope you all enjoy."

A woman with short brown hair entered wearing a long print skirt and hand-embroidered blouse. She said, "Buenos dias, my name is Carmen Sonnes. Thank you for inviting me to join your group today. Forgive me if I take a moment to set up."

"I appreciate you coming on such short notice," Jake said as the woman approached them.

On one side of the room, Carmen placed three pictures on easels. "Mr. Walton is playing humble. I don't know an artist who would not have boarded the private jet he sent for me."

"Please, call me Jake." Jake smiled smoothly back at the woman and directed his next comment to Lil. "I met Carmen at an art exhibit in Austin a few years ago. I thought you might enjoy meeting her, also."

Over the last week, contained to her apartment, it was easy to forget that Jake was a man of immense power and influence. He didn't wave his wealth around like some war banner trophy as Dominic did. Instead, it was an integral part of who he was and how he interacted with the world around him. Lil doubted that Jake had wondered at all if Carmen would accept his invitation. What was it like to be so used to winning that desired outcomes were hardly a surprise?

"From what I've been told this is a mother/child art group ranging from six months to two years old?" Carmen asked.

"Yes," the instructor said. "We use edible finger paints and a variety of paper types to allow our young participants to explore the textures and colors of art."

"And what do the mothers usually do?" Carmen asked.

One mother laughed and said, "We manage the chaos."

Carmen waved a few young people from the doorway. "I hope you'll accept some assistance in that role today, because I'd really like everyone to be engaged."

A handful of male and female college aged "assistants" came to stand at the table with the mothers. Each one had a wooden easel box full of everything from oil paints and brushes to art sticks and charcoal pencils. "Please accept these art supplies as a gift from me to you. Inside your box you will find a variety of tools you could use to perform the task I will set for you. Keep it simple. You'll have about an hour to complete your project. Before we can truly teach art to our children, we must experience it ourselves."

Six easels were set up with a blank canvas just a foot or so behind each child.

Jake's smile faltered when one student handed him a box of art supplies. "No, thank you," he said.

Lil smiled over her shoulder at Jake. "You're not getting

off the hook that easily. If I'm doing this, so are you."

Jake inspected the contents of the box doubtfully. He set his easel directly beside Lil's.

Carmen said, "I didn't study art formally so this may be an atypical lesson for some of you. Today is not about learning a specific technique but will hopefully be interesting to you regardless of your various abilities. Today we will explore your artistic voice."

As she spoke, the instructor handed out multiple baby jars filled with brightly colored paint to the college students who opened them and began to work with the infants.

"I brought three pictures with me today that I feel represent my voice. My style and my art have been called many things: Mexican, Latino, Tejano, Chicano, Tex-Mex, Mexican-American, contemporary, modern, woman-centered, figurative, and representational." Carmen smiled. "I suppose my work is some or all of these things. Basically, it is just what my heart and mind dream up. I am my art and my art is me. I am passionate about color and fascinated by Mexico." She pointed to one of the easels. "The first painting is called *Listening to My Own Counsel*. When we reach a difficult crossroad, we sometimes go looking for answers outside ourselves. The answers are almost always within us. The four black birds represent the voices and advice of others. The woman turns her gaze and ears inward, beneath her blanket. The blue feather represents traditional wisdom. Symbolism is one way to express yourself in your art. The second painting is called *Manitas*." She lovingly laid a hand on the top of the second painting. "*Manita* is short for *hermanita* or little sister in Spanish. This is how we fondly refer to our sisters and girlfriends. I portray two women, sisters, back to back and on the lookout for each other. I symbolize their tight unity and entangled love by weaving their hair into one thick braid, which runs down the center of the painting." She moved to stand beside the last easel. "The third and final work is called *Esperanza*. It is a pencil drawing and one of my earliest works. It is my interpretation of a handful of stories passed down through the generations, from my great-grandmother, to my grandmother, to my mother and lastly to me." Carmen's expression creased with sorrow as if she were experiencing the pain depicted in the artwork. "This story is of the hardships the people endured during the war, particularly the women. Wives often accompanied their husbands to war to carry ammunition, cook, wash, and tend to the injured. Nursing infants and those born on the battlefields became part of those camps. At nighttime, when enemy troops were near it was imperative for the survival of all that the hungry babies be kept quiet. When breasts ran dry, desperate mothers stuck stones, clods of dirt and even bullets in the wailing child's mouth. Some inconsolable babies had to be smothered. The magnitude of this tale imprinted on my mind as a child and I tell it in this pencil drawing."

A couple of the women teared up at the description of the last image. One woman said with disgust, "I would never hurt my child, no matter what."

Carmen shook her head sadly. "If you can say that, you have never seen war up close. And before you judge, ask yourself—are we so different from our ancestors?" She looked each woman proudly in the eye, holding their attention and pulling at their emotions. "We still give our children to war every day when we send our young men and women into battle on foreign soils. Are our older sons and daughters less precious than our infants? Is that loss any less heart-wrenching than the one in my story?" She took a deep breath, regaining the calm with which she had entered the room. "Still, embrace the reaction you felt to my story. Express it on canvas today. Art is not about everyone having the same vision or shared history – it's about finding your message, your voice, and exposing it to the world. So, no matter what anyone draws today, accept it because it is an intimate look into their souls and therefore should be honored as such."

"Damn," Jake whispered to Lil. "Now I can't draw stick figures."

Lil wiped a rogue tear from her cheek and smiled at him. "You could if your soul is full of sticks."

"What if I draw you naked?" His words tickled her ear.

Lil wagged a finger at him. "Try it and you invite serious payback."

Carmen smiled and said, "Enough chatter. Choose your tools. Take a moment to look inside yourself instead of at the blank canvas. When you are ready, put a piece of yourself onto the canvas. Tell your story."

The room was charged with emotion. Even the babies seemed to sense that something important was happening and were subdued as they dunked their fingers into the edible paints and mixed colors onto the papers before them.

Lil chose colorful art sticks.

Jake chose black charcoal pencils.

Lil dove into drawing with bold lines and bright colors.

Jake's moves were more precise and calculated. He drew himself on top of a mountain surrounded by several doors. Behind each door was a path that led to a different destination. One led to a cliff. One led to a place of order and straight, bold lines. Another led to a much less clear picture. Jake reached over and borrowed a few of Lil's art sticks even though he could have easily used his own. He drew a simple woman with a child and surrounded both with a wild assortment of colors. It was the only place where color touched his sketch.

He caught Lil watching with fascination and actually blushed. "That's how you make me feel," he said simply.

Lil almost knocked over her box of supplies, catching it at the last second. She looked at her own sketch and wondered what he thought of the fact that she hadn't included him in it at all. She had drawn herself, serious and determined, looking miserable with Colby clutched in her arms while she chased Abby. She wasn't even entirely sure what the scene meant, only that it had poured out of her and now stared back at her, revealing something she wasn't sure she wanted to discuss with Jake.

Jake studied her sketch for a moment and said, "Don't take an office job, Lil."

She searched his face.

"You're already the mother Colby needs."

Lil looked quickly at her child, who was licking the green paint off one finger, then back to Jake. "I'm not, Jake. I haven't been the person I need to be, but I am changing that." She thought about how part of becoming a better person had involved killing any chance that something real could develop between them. Forgetting, even for a moment, that her friends were using this time to access Jake's private accounts would only lead to more heartache. She had to remember that none of this was real. "The older I get the more I wonder if anyone has the answers or if, like me, they are just doing the best they can and praying every day that it's enough."

The seriousness of her response set Jake back on his heels. He opened and closed his mouth without saying a word.

Carmen had gone from mother to mother and discussed each creation with the novice artists, until she came to Jake and Lil. She correctly interpreted the tension between the two and took them by surprise by reaching out and taking each of them by one hand. For an uncomfortable moment, she simply held them and then nodded without saying anything, giving each hand a comforting squeeze before letting go.

Carmen returned to the front of the group and began to share her observations, but Lil wasn't listening. She was lost in her reaction to Jake's sketch and in his response to hers. Of course, someone like him would think she had options besides taking a job she already dreaded, but that only highlighted how little they had in common. Although it was flattering to be considered someone who added color to his life, she'd already made her choice.

His picture would have been quite different had she confessed the real reason they were together that day. Would it have shown her being led to the gallows? Or, just as painful, would she simply not have shown up at all?

How did betrayal look in charcoal?

Colby let out a cry of frustration and Lil had never been so happy to have an event interrupted.

"She's probably hungry," Lil said as she headed toward her child. She used the supplies provided to clean Colby off and put her back in her stroller, then gave her address to the instructor who said the artwork would be mailed to her.

The visiting artist approached her. "Lil, right?"

"Yes," she said, not really wanting to engage in a conversation with someone who had seen more than she showed most people.

"Your work was very moving," Carmen said.

Lil dismissed the comment as polite small talk. "Thank you. I've always enjoyed sketching, just for fun. Nothing serious."

Carmen continued, "You captured a lot of emotion in just a few crisp lines. You have a gift. You might want to explore it."

Anger flooded in and added bite to Lil's words. "I'm taking a different road; one that I'm happy about."

The artist did not waver. "Honor the message you heard today, both from yourself and your man."

"He's not . . ."

Carmen smiled and shook her head. "Art never lies."

Unlike me, Lil wanted to say.

Alethea and Jeremy had better be finished whatever the heck they were doing because she needed to end this date. It was simply too painful.

LIL WAS DOUBLE-CHECKING that she had everything she'd come with when Jake walked over to join her. Lil said, "Well, this was . . ." She paused. *Painful? Awful? Torture?* "Nice," she finished lamely.

He rolled one of her loose curls around his finger. "When I imagined this date last night, you were smiling at this point."

Lil tried but failed.

Confusion swirled within her. Was she hoping Jake was innocent so she could believe the side of him that he was showing her today? Or that he was guilty so she would feel less awful about what she'd done? Neither outcome held much comfort for her.

He put an arm gently around her waist and together they thanked everyone and exited the room. Jake guided her out of the building and onto the sidewalk. "Are you ready for lunch?" he asked.

"I really should be getting home. Colby will need a bottle and a nap . . ."

With his arm still around Lil, Jake said, "Just one more place. Then I promise to deposit you back at your penthouse. Do you have formula with you?"

She considered making an excuse why she couldn't go,

but today was already more of a lie than she could stomach. "Yes."

"Let's walk then," Jake said.

They stopped in front of the Isabella Stewart Gardner Museum, the once private home of a woman who had collected art from all over the world and donated the building along with her collection to the city. Although the building had undergone renovations and modern additions had been added, Jake led her to an old entrance.

"Have you been here before?" he asked as they entered the museum and were instantly met by someone who ushered them down a dark hallway and through various rooms that were filled with an eclectic and mostly unlabeled art collection. Normally Lil would have asked to stop to savor some of the many works, but she was determined to end this day at the first opportunity.

When the inner courtyard came into view she almost forgot everything beyond its beauty. Stepping into the long, rectangular courtyard revealed the true outstanding Italian-styled palazzo that had once been nothing more than a private home of a very eccentric and wealthy woman. The garden was a visual feast of flowers, statues, and old-world architecture. Elegantly dressed staff met them as they entered the area and led them to a sole table set up at one end of the courtyard, hidden from public view by flowers but positioned so that once seated they would still have an incredible view of the area. Candles lit what would have otherwise been a darkened corner.

Lil had heard of the museum before and the quirky history of the woman who had built it and then donated the building to the city. She'd always meant to come see it, but somehow never had. She was reasonably certain, however, that the courtyard was normally closed to the public. Of course it wasn't closed to Jake. She didn't imagine many places in the world were.

Colby's needs overshadowed the romance of the location at first. Lil sought a place to change her, then asked the staff to help her prepare a bottle. Jake sat across from Lil, appearing to wait patiently while she fed her daughter and then settled her down into the stroller for a nap.

When Lil finally settled back into her seat, she expected Jake to be irritated with her, but found him looking rather pleased with himself instead. He said, "I had a cook prepare a meal for us. I hope you like beef tenderloin. Normally, I would ask for your preference, but it would have ruined the surprise."

He accepted a glass of wine from the staff, tasted it and nodded in acceptance of it. "Do you like it?" He gestured with the glass to the area around them. The server offered to fill Lil's glass, but she shook her head. The last thing she needed was to relax her tongue.

Do I like it?

The setting was unimaginably beautiful, the staff was attentive yet unobtrusive, and the space provided enough quiet for her daughter to sleep while they ate. Who wouldn't love being treated like visiting royalty?

Only a woman who had no right to enjoy it.

She couldn't look him in the eye. "It's beautiful," she

said.

He took both of her hands in his and waited for her to look up from the table. When she finally did he said, "Why do I get the feeling that there is something wrong?"

"Today was beautiful, Jake. I mean that. The way you included Colby into our day together . . ." She motioned to the garden around them and the staff that perked up as soon as her hand raised. "All this . . ."

"Your daughter is your priority." His expression held a bit of longing.

Why are you making this so hard? "You have to see how this wouldn't work."

"Why? Because I don't love you?"

Ouch.

Lil pulled her hands out of his. "There's that."

He opened his napkin and placed it on his lap. "Love is a myth perpetuated by people who don't have anything better to believe in. You're fantastic in bed, you make me laugh, and I enjoy your company. That's enough for me."

Sadly, he probably meant what he was saying.

"That sounds like the last, valiant declaration of a man about to lose his heart completely," she scoffed.

Instead of brushing her comment off or picking up the challenge, he gave her that steady, unblinking look she was beginning to understand meant that his mind was set to his course. "Maybe," he answered.

More on the subject was interrupted by the food arriving. Delicious as it looked, Lil couldn't imagine putting anything into her churning stomach. She finally toyed with a piece of beef enough to bring it to her lips.

"Move in with me," he said calmly.

Lil dropped the fork to her plate with a loud clatter along with the meat she hadn't tasted. "We discussed this."

The strong set of his jaw and the proud look in his eyes told her that he wasn't going to let her brush the topic aside. "Not because you might be pregnant. Move in because you want to fall asleep in my arms at night and wake up next to me each morning."

Lil hedged, "I have Colby . . ."

He said, "Don't hide behind her. You know I could more than take care of both of you. She would have the best of everything."

Except his love and what kind of life would that be for either of them? "For how long?" Lil asked.

He shrugged. "If you're looking for promises, I don't have any. If it's your financial future you're worried about, I'll have my lawyers draw up some sort of settlement to remove that concern."

There's the Jake I know. Lil tossed her napkin onto the table and stood. "Wow, you're about as romantic as my car service plan."

"Sit down. Lil," he said in a tone that probably worked on people who cared about pleasing him.

Lil was unimpressed. She leaned one hand onto the table and looked him straight in the eye. "No, I will not sit down. Did you seriously just offer me a settlement to ease my pain on the day—whichever day you choose—when you throw me out?"

His explanation was lacking. "It's quite common to think about . . ."

Lil gathered her purse, took her baby stroller by the handle and started to leave. So as not to disturb Colby, she lowered her voice, but her tone remained angry. "Maybe it's common in your world. Not mine. I'm one of those poor sops, I suppose, who has nothing better to believe in than . . . than . . ."

He blocked her exit. "You can't even say the word and you think I'm the one with the problem?"

She sucked a breath in harshly, her hands flexing on the handle of her stroller. "Fine. You're right. I'm too screwed up to accept your offer. Luckily for you, there are probably a hundred women within yelling distance who would jump at your offer. Ask one of them. Now get out of my way."

"I don't want them." His jaw set, he planted his feet and continued to block her path. "I want you."

Lil could be just as stubborn. "We all want things we can't have, Jake. That's reality. Now, seriously, don't make me ask someone for help to get past you."

He stepped aside. "I'll drive you home," he growled.

"No," she said and held a hand in front of him. "You'll give me my keys and find your own ride to wherever you're going—hopefully New York."

Smooth Jake was struggling to contain his growing frustration with her. Impatiently he dug the keys out of the front pocket of his shorts, but did not immediately give them to her. "If you're sure that is what you want."

Lil simply maintained her stance. What she wanted

didn't matter; she knew what she had to do. She wanted to throw herself into his arms, tell him everything, and accept his pitiful offer. She wanted to believe that despite what he said, he was already half in love with her. And against all common sense, she wanted to think that he could forgive her if she told him the truth.

Wanting wasn't enough.

And it certainly didn't make his last offer any less insulting.

"Lil," he said and paused as his cell phone rang. He checked it quickly. "I have to take this."

Unable to stop herself, she said, "Maybe it's your lawyer and you can tell him to leave the name blank for now on that settlement form."

His phone rang again. He answered his phone, but mouthed to Lil, "This is not over."

Yes, it is, Lil thought. *I'm not doing this again.*

She was almost through the roped area that led to the rest of the museum when she heard Jake completely lose his cool for the first time since she'd met him. His voice boomed through the courtyard. "What the hell? I thought you'd beefed up our firewall in anticipation of something like this. I'm absolutely coming back—right now. And I'm going to find out how this happened."

Lil stepped up her pace.

Shit. Shit. Shit.

THIS WAS EXACTLY why he didn't believe in acting impulsively.

He should have been in New York, in his office, on top of the situation and keeping his team on high alert. There was absolutely no excuse for something like this happening, but there was an explanation.

He'd let his lust for Lil cloud his judgment and distract him when he most needed to be focused on saving Corisi Enterprises.

I'm no better than Dominic. We both deserve to be flipping burgers next year if we screw this up.

What was it about those Dartley women?

For just a moment, he entertained the possibility that they could have been planted by the competition. Did Stephan's initial plot against Dominic include gaining their trust and then taking both men out of the picture via the oldest trick in the book?

No, not only were Lil and Abby likely the most thoroughly background checked women in the country, but he pictured Lil putting him in his place the very first night he'd met her and smiled. Lil would make an awful mole. She said whatever was on her mind. She might be frustrating as hell—but she was no liar.

The weight of responsibility lay squarely on his shoulders. He'd watched Dominic check out of reality after he lost his father over a month ago and there was no sign that he'd be checking back in any time soon.

Getting involved with Lil right now was irresponsible, ill-advised, and all he'd been able to think about this past week. Why couldn't she just move in with him and remove the fascination of it all? Familiarity was the most likely antidote to what was beginning to feel like an obsession.

Mentioning the settlement had been a mistake. She was wavering until he'd tossed that tidbit into the ring.

Maladroit comments were out of character for him. So was asking a woman to move in with him; never mind practically begging her to.

What was happening to him?

He wasn't sure how to move forward with Lil.

He had no idea how to make Dominic see how close they were to losing everything.

But there was one area he was still certain of. He was going to find out who had hacked into his personal computer and whoever it was he was going to crush them financially, and quite possibly, physically. Never before had he understood the lure of violence, but right about now the urge to punch someone was surging within him.

PULLING UP TO the building that housed her new apartment, Lil decided that it was too beautiful of a day to hide away inside so she handed her keys to the valet and took her daughter to a local park. She was pushing Colby lightly back and forth in one of the baby swings when her phone rang.

She almost didn't answer it.

What am I afraid of? Really, how much worse could today get?

Alethea's voice exploded from the phone as soon as Lil answered. "Lil, I've got good news for you."

Considering the source, that was highly unlikely.

"I could use some, Al." Lil sighed and pushed her daughter's swing again.

"I don't think they're doing anything illegal. Everything points more to damage control. Looks like our friends are in scramble mode to fix something. My guess is it has something to do with that Chinese server Dominic has scheduled to unveil next month. Jake's good, though. Nothing in his email was specific."

"So the good news is that Dominic is having some huge server issue?" It didn't sound like anything to celebrate.

"No the good news is that my instincts are still sharp. There is definitely something going on, but it doesn't sound like anything that will endanger your sister."

So Jake isn't a criminal.

Lil scrambled to piece together what it all meant. How would their date this morning have ended if she'd never doubted him? Could she blame Jake for thinking their relationship might not last when she ended every encounter with him by telling him that she never wanted to see him again?

I keep thinking that Jake is the one who is wrong, the one who has to change, but what if it's me? What if I could have had everything but lost it because I was too scared to trust that something that wonderful could happen to me? Never knowing the answer to that would be the price she'd pay for believing the worst of Jake again and again. "I'm heading down to New York in the morning. I've changed my mind. I don't think you should go." Lil balanced the phone on her shoulder while she released her daughter from the swing and returned her to the stroller.

Lil was too restless to stand there and pretend she wasn't full of nervous energy.

Real concern entered her friend's voice. "Are you feeling guilty about today? We didn't have a choice, Lil."

Everyone faced tough choices, but not everyone always made the wrong one. "Al, Jake knows someone hacked his computer."

"What? How do you know?" Alethea's voice went up a pitch.

Back on the sidewalk and heading home, Lil said, "He got a phone call while we were at lunch and I heard him say that they had made changes to their firewall to ensure that something like this couldn't happen. What if he knows it was Jeremy? What if he traces it back to him . . . to you . . . to me?"

Alethea said, "Jeremy did say that he'd encountered a snag."

"A snag? A snag?" Lil heard her own voice rise with panic and took a deep breath. People on the street were beginning to stare at her. *Great, maybe I'll end up in a video on the internet and round this week out.* She lowered her voice to near a whisper. "You said no one would ever know."

"Knowing that someone breached your security is a long way from knowing who did it. Jeremy is careful. He has several dummy, dead-end accounts. No one will ever find out about today, Lil, unless you tell them."

"I know," Lil said with little conviction as she gratefully ducked into the privacy of the high-rise building she still didn't consider her home. She leaned her head back against the cold wall of the elevator as it carried her up to the top floor.

"Lil, I recognize that tone. You want to confess."

"I know I can't."

"Exactly. Jeremy and I could be in serious trouble with the law if you do. This is the kind of secret to take with you to the grave, Lil."

"Don't you think I know that?" *Only a fool would want to risk everything for a man who'd made it pretty clear that he didn't love her.* Lil let herself into her penthouse.

Alethea shared her opinion by saying nothing at all.

Lil removed Colby from the stroller and took her to the bedroom to change her. The contrast between the mundane and the insane made it difficult to reconcile the two. Lil said, "Trust me, if I didn't spill the beans this morning, I can keep my mouth shut through anything."

"That bad?" Despite the tension of their conversation, Alethea sounded sympathetic.

"That good. He even asked me to move in with him."

"What did you say?"

Lil grimaced. "I said no. What could I say?"

"Were you tempted?"

"I don't know. He says the stupidest things, but then he does something that shows me that he cares about what's important to me and I want to believe that something is possible between us. Oh, Al, I think I'm falling in love with him, but I ruined everything, didn't I?"

Ever the practical one, Alethea said, "You can have your happy ending, Lil, if we mutually agree to forget what we did today."

Lil had done plenty in her life that she considered rash, but she'd never hidden. When you are doing something that you believe in, you don't have to hide—at least, that was what she'd always believed.

Deceiving Jake ranked highest on her list of what she regretted doing. Looking back over her time with him, it was clear to Lil that he'd tried to protect her—even from their attraction. Not telling him was a blackness growing in her heart. "I don't feel right about lying, Al."

All sympathy left her friend's voice. "How right will you feel when we're sharing a cell at the local penitentiary? It won't be only me going down. You're just as culpable."

I know.

Lil said slowly, "Maybe Jake would understand why we had to know what was going on."

"Or maybe not." Alethea blew out an exasperated breath. "We're not kids anymore, Lil. No one is going to lock us up for one night and try to scare us straight. We all have too much to lose. Do you want Abby to raise Colby for you? Because that's what will happen if you forget how serious this is and end up in the slammer with me."

Lil shuddered at the thought and confused tears made it difficult to locate the wipes as she changed her daughter's soiled diaper. When she'd agreed to the hack, she hadn't thought this far ahead. She'd risked much more than she'd understood at the time. Colby was her number one priority. How could she have done something that put her in jeopardy?

She secured the new diaper, arranged her daughter's clothing and hugged her daughter to her as she walked back to the living room.

"I have to go see Jeremy and warn him," Alethea said.

"See if he can cover his tracks better?" Lil asked, settling Colby on the floor with some toys.

"That, and to warn him that they know someone was there. He planned to go back in one more time."

"Back in? Why?"

"He said he found something he hadn't expected to and it made him curious."

"Oh, no. Alethea, he'll get caught for sure if he tries to access their system again."

"That's why I've got to go to his house. He doesn't answer his phone most of the time—not even texts."

Lying on one side on the floor, Lil forced a smile for her daughter's sake. Colby wasn't fooled, she let out a loud wail. *I totally know how you feel, Colby.* In a shaky voice, Lil asked, "Al, this is going to work out, isn't it?"

Alethea answered with more bravado than she likely felt. "It all depends how smart your boyfriend is."

Shit.

Lil remembered reading a magazine that estimated Jake's IQ to be around the 190 range. He might be irritatingly sexy, frustratingly stubborn, and emotionally thrifty, but there was no doubt that Jake was brilliant.

Oh, this is going to go really badly.

Maybe it was time to start being extra nice to her future brother-in-law. He might be the only one able to keep her and her friends out of jail.

Chapter Twelve

A
LTHOUGH, LIL HAD arrived mid-day, she and Abby hadn't said more than a few sentences to each other. Lil had claimed fatigue from the short flight and had retreated with Colby to the suite Dominic's staff had prepared for them.

A set of five rooms, two bedrooms, dressing room, lounging room and bathroom were all perfectly stocked with everything Lil could imagine she or her baby could possibly need. Abby showed her an intercom on the wall and instructed her to use it if she needed anything. A cleaning woman, a nanny, and a stylist were all on location and on call for Lil if she wanted to use any of them that weekend.

"I'll be fine," Lil had said.

Abby had searched her face, noted the strain around her eyes and asked, "Are you sure everything is ok, Lil? You know you can tell me anything."

"I'm just tired."

Abby had hesitated. "If you're still worried about the interview, don't be. No one blamed you for that and you handled it perfectly. Dominic said he was impressed."

The interview? Wow, that felt like a lifetime ago. If only that were still my greatest concern.

"I said I was tired." She hadn't meant to sound as harsh as she had.

Abby looked a bit sad suddenly, which did nothing to improve Lil's mood. "Of course. Get some rest. Dinner is at six. The Andrades are joining us. I hope you're feeling better by then."

Lil turned away from her sister and said angrily, "I won't embarrass you, if that's what you're worried about."

Abby sighed, a clear sign that she wanted to say more but wouldn't. "I'm glad you're here, Lil." She closed the door softly behind her as she left.

I don't know how you could be.

I'm ruining everything—just like I always do.

Colby looked sadly up at her mother.

"Don't say it, Colby," Lil said.

WITH HER DAUGHTER down for a perfectly timed nap, Lil was able to shower and slip into an oversized white terrycloth robe. She'd scheduled the nanny for six o'clock, but for now Lil felt better having Colby with her.

A clothing rack had arrived after Abby had left; each hanger on it held a more beautiful dress than the last. Gift boxes full of designer shoes, hair accessories and jewelry had accompanied the delivery. Under different circumstances, Lil might have actually enjoyed trying the dresses on, but guilt hung heavy on her mind. There had to be a way she could fix this.

A loud knock on the suite's outer door made her jump. Was it Jake?

I'm not ready to see him yet.

She braced herself and opened the door.

Impressively dressed in what Lil guessed was an Armani suit—Abby said it was his favorite designer, Dominic Corisi filled her doorway. He was Jake's height, and perfectly groomed, but reminded Lil a bit of a restless tiger at a zoo. If it weren't for his blatant devotion to her sister, Lil would have closed the door instead of pretending to be happy to see him. He had a reputation for being ruthless and the entire world had recently witnessed how he considered himself a bit above the law's reproach when it came to what he wanted.

He was definitely a man that even Lil wanted to stay on the good side of. This was no high school bully; this man wielded more power than many dynasties could boast.

Why did I think we could ever get away with hacking into the emails of men like this?

"May I come in?" Dominic asked.

Lil looked down at her robe. It covered more than any dress on that rack would, so she nodded and stepped back from the door.

He studied her face for a moment and said, "Abby said you weren't feeling well."

Understatement of the year.

Is this where he threatens me because my poor attitude is a dark cloud on a supposedly otherwise happy weekend? Lil moved to stand behind a chair, using it to support her suddenly unsteady legs. "It's nothing serious."

Dominic crossed the room to look out the window and spoke while taking in the view. "I love your sister, Lil. I'm going to marry her."

And you're here to make sure I don't mess it up?

Lil swallowed nervously. "I know."

He turned from the window and frowned. "That makes you a sort of little sister to me. I want you to feel comfortable here."

His words floored Lil. When she didn't view him through the lens of her guilt, he looked more uncomfortable than he did threatening. "I do," she lied softly.

He buried both hands in the pants pockets of his suit; certainly not the mannerism of a man with ill intentions. He continued gruffly, "If anything was ever bothering you, you could tell me and I would move Heaven and Earth to fix it for you. You know that, right? I protect what is mine."

He'd come to offer her his support? Lil's eyes filled with tears that she angrily blinked away. This was the Dominic her sister had described to her, the one who was fiercely loyal to those he cared about. Was it possible that he not only loved her sister, but would really consider Lil part of his family? If so, maybe confessing was actually the best course she could take. A man like Dominic would understand breaking the rules to keep someone you care about safe. Lil asked, "Have you ever done anything that felt like the right thing to do at the time, but as soon as it was done, you regretted it and would do anything to undo it?"

Dominic conceded ruefully, "I'm unfortunately familiar with that feeling."

Lil came out from behind the chair and approached him. "If making things right meant putting someone you cared deeply about at risk, would you? What do you do when none of the options are good ones?"

Dominic straightened, unpocketing his hands and clenching them at his sides. "Is this about Jake?"

Jake was definitely one of the reasons she wanted to turn back the clock and not involve Alethea and Jeremy. Slow tears began to pour down Lil's cheeks and she sank into one of the chairs. She couldn't put a voice to the fears that roared within her.

I can handle a broken heart, please, just let the consequences be mine alone.

Don't let me ruin the happiness my sister has finally found.

Don't let me have put my friends in danger.

Please, she begged the universe, I'll mind my business from now on.

I don't want Abby to raise Colby.

Dominic came to stand beside her chair and patted the back of her bowed head awkwardly. Lil continued to sob softly, trying but not succeeding to muster the strength to tell him everything.

Dominic asked, "Did he sleep with you?"

His question took her off guard and she answered too honestly, "It's not about that."

Dominic withdrew his hand and his roar boomed through the room. "I'm going to kill him."

The door slammed behind him as he stormed out of the suite.

Lil raised her head, sniffed, and gripped the arm of her chair with one hand while wiping the tears off one of her cheeks with her other.

Well, that went well.

JAKE HAD JUST arrived at the Corisi home for dinner when he saw his friend charging down the hallway toward him, looking like he wanted to hurt someone. Had he heard about the most recent breach to their security?

Dominic grabbed Jake by one suit lapel and hauled him toward him. "I'm going to kill you."

Normally, Dominic appropriately reserved his fury for those who had perpetrated the offense. Jake knocked his friend's hand off of him. "Calm down, Dom. They didn't get anything. I'm careful with what I put in my emails. And I've had my team working on it since yesterday. No one is getting back in."

Dominic looked like he was about to reach for Jake again, but stopped suddenly. "What are you talking about?"

Jake adjusted his rumpled jacket and stalled. "What are *you* talking about?"

Dominic paced in front of Jake, his hands flexing in a threatening manner at his sides. He growled, "You slept with Lil."

"Oh, Lil." Maybe Dominic didn't know about the breach yet. Normally he would have informed him immediately, but the hacker had targeted Jake's emails and that made it personal. Jake wanted to catch this rat himself.

"Don't play dumb. Yes, Lil. I sent you down there to

make sure she was safe."

"I told you not to send me. I said—"

Dominic stopped, stood nose-to-nose with Jake and accused, "Whatever you said, you left out the part where you were going to break one of the fundamental rules of friendship."

Don't let your crazy friend lose his company because you're too busy chasing a skirt?

Jake became impatient with his friend's melodramatic fixation on something that was none of his business. He spoke calmly, rationally, hoping some of it would rub off on his friend. "I did exactly what you asked me to. I moved her into her new place. Don't be a hypocrite."

Dominic ran a hand through his hair with frustration. He leaned in and said, "I still think I have to kill you."

Jake held his ground, mocking Dominic instead of cowering to him as he supposed some would. They had spent too many years together for Jake to ever fear him. Brute strength rarely won over intelligence. "What did you think would happen when you sent me up there? You knew I liked her."

Fire flew from his friend's eyes, but he kept his hands to himself, perhaps sensing that Jake was more than ready to retaliate. He frowned. "I don't know, I thought you'd take her out a few times. A nice date. Movies maybe. What happened to treating a woman with respect?"

Jake couldn't contain the laugh Dominic's comment inspired. "You *kidnapped* Abby."

Dom turned away and began pacing again. "That's different. People expect that from me. I trusted you."

Jake shrugged and threw angry suggestions at his friend. "Maybe it's time you stop trusting me. Maybe I can't be responsible for saving your ass anymore. What if I am just as screwed up as you are?"

Anger left Dominic in a whoosh and a ridiculous smile spread across his face. "You love her," he said with a smirk.

Jake took a step back and denied it. "No, I don't."

Dominic advanced, his smile only growing wider as he counted off his observations on his fingers. "She's crying. You're miserable. Maddy is right; this is working." Dominic folded his arms across his chest benevolently. "I forgive you because I know what it's like to want a woman so badly that you are willing to risk everything." His expression turned serious and he said, "You know you have to marry her, though."

Forget about a shotgun wedding, Dominic would proba-bly use an armed military drone. Jake smiled at the thought. That slip earned an angry glare from Dom and a threat.

Dominic said, "Don't make me tell Marie."

Classic Dom—go straight for the big guns. It was a pleasure to take that option away from him. "She already knows."

Dominic straightened with rage. "You told her? What the hell were you thinking? I'm going to hope that it was because you realized the gravity of what you've done and wanted her advice on how to do the right thing." He looked like he wanted to wrap his hands around Jake's neck, but controlled himself, satisfying himself with a warning. "In case I'm not being clear enough—plan a wedding or plan a funeral. Your choice."

Abby stuck her head through the door and called to Dominic. "Dom, the Andrades just pulled in. Are you ready?"

With one final glare, Dominic announced, "Yes, I think Jake and I understand each other now."

Perfectly, Jake thought.

And, for once, he agreed with Dominic. He shouldn't have slept with his best friend's future sister-in-law, but now that he had—marrying her was the only course that made sense. Lil would agree with him, once he explained it to her. For the sake of her child, she needed permanency and security. He could offer her that. He *would* offer that—as soon as he could get her to talk to him again.

As LIL SAT at the outrageously long dining room table, she smoothed the material of the conservative green dress she'd chosen. The crisp lines and modest neckline boosted her confidence. Tonight was not about her and Jake, nor was it about the emotional baggage Lil had packed for the trip—it was about her sister and celebrating her finding love. Green was a peaceful color, one that could blend in and stay out of trouble.

Dominic and Abby were seated at one end of the table, happily absorbed in a private conversation. Dominic's sister, Nicole and her fiancé, Stephan, were seated next to Abby. Lil spared a moment to envy how Nicole always looked like she belonged on the cover of *Vogue*.

Lil was surprised to see that Stephan had brought his parents, his aunt and uncle, and if Lil was correct—even one of his cousins and her French husband. Abby had said that she and Dominic had been spending time with the Andrades lately, but Lil hadn't realized that they had gotten this close.

Dominic's personal assistant, Mrs. Duhamel, smiled at Lil from directly across the table. Lil tried to return the smile, gave up and looked down at her plate instead. One of the most powerful women in China, billionairess Zhang Yajun, sat at Lil's left. Normally, Lil would have bombarded her with questions about what her life was like, but tonight Lil was determined to hold her tongue and quietly blend into this collection of some of the world's richest people.

If you don't say anything, you can't say anything wrong.

Jake took the seat to her right and touched her arm to gain her attention. He kept his voice at an intimate volume. "Lil, we need to talk."

"No, we don't," she hissed back in somewhat of a whisper.

Dominic stood and the table fell silent. "Thank you all for coming tonight." He took a moment to smile at each person at the table then he reached down, took Abby by the hand, and encouraged her to stand beside him. With one arm around her waist, he said, "If anyone had told me a couple months ago that you would all be gathered to celebrate the formal announcement of our engagement, I would have thought they were crazy. But here we are and I am honored to call you friends."

Approval was expressed in a variety of voices and languages.

Abby clasped her hands in front of her, the only indication that she wasn't entirely comfortable speaking before the group. "Helping Nicole go through her father's things, inspired me to take a second look at old photo albums and what little still remains of my own parents' things. I found a poem that my mother wrote when we were children. It seemed appropriate to read in honor of how our family has extended in the most wonderful ways."

She took out a folded and faded piece of paper and started to read:

Real love is not like a pizza
With two slices for some
One for others
And nothing left for the unlucky
Real love is like a fountain
Joyously spilling over
Where there is always more than enough
For those who need it
And it is just as generous
To those who return to it
As to those who never left

Lil's eyes welled at the wisdom of the mother she still missed, even as rogue thoughts plagued her. How did real love feel toward a little accidental water contamination? That was the question she needed answered.

Dominic hugged Abby to his side and the table was oddly quiet for a moment. Nicole turned and said something softly to her fiancé. Stephan smiled down at her and nodded.

Nicole addressed her brother. "Dom, invite her for to-morrow. I'll be fine."

There was a wave of happy gasps from those around her.

Dominic asked, "Are you sure, Nicole?"

His sister considered it for a moment then nodded with a teary smile. "I want the fountain." Stephan hugged her and whispered something into her ear that made her blush.

Abby leaned down and hugged her future sister-in-law, and then said, "I promise to keep this short so we can eat, but when we make the formal announcement of our engagement tomorrow the house will be full. I wanted to ask something in the privacy of the ones we're closest to." She looked around the table and said, "Nicole, Maddy, Zhang,— I'd like for you to be my bridesmaids. You don't have to answer now, I just wanted to tell you that nothing would mean more to me than having you up there when I marry Dominic. It's happening in three weeks, so you'd be committing to a bit of a whirlwind wedding, but Dominic assures me it can be done."

Nicole and Maddy left their seats to hug Abby.

Lil noticed that Zhang's expression remained carefully polite. She neither accepted nor declined the request.

Abby walked over to where Lil was sitting and asked, "Lil, will you be my maid of honor?"

The room spun behind her and Lil suddenly felt sick. She didn't know anything about high-class weddings and assuming that type of responsibility sounded like a recipe for disaster. Lil shook her head with uncertainty. "I don't know."

Abby's hurt expression tore at Lil, especially when her sister pleaded, "You're my sister, Lil. I love you. Say you'll stand beside me that day."

I've done more than enough damage already. The closer Lil got to her sister and her future brother in law, the more that went wrong. Abby would be better off choosing any of the other women at the table. Panic temporarily overwhelmed her. Lil stood, her chair toppling behind her, and said, "I can't."

Giving in to a true moment of cowardice, Lil ran from the stunned expressions on the faces of everyone at the table.

DOMINIC LEANED FORWARD, one hand clenching on the table and the other pointing across the table at Jake. "This is your fault. Fix it," he ordered.

Jake folded his arms across his chest. "Your family. You fix it."

Dominic left his spot at the head of the table and strode toward Jake. "It's going to be your family, too, if you know what is good for you."

Surging from his seat, Jake met his friend half way. "Or what? What are you going to do, Dominic? Hit me? Try it."

Abby sprinted toward them, but Mrs. Duhamel stopped her with a hand on one of her arms before she reached them. "They need to settle this themselves, Abby," she said.

Dominic swung at Jake's jaw, but Jake avoided the hit and landed one of his own in Dominic's abdomen. The sound of the breath leaving Dominic was a hiss in an otherwise silent room.

Jake addressed the doubled-over Dominic. "I'm tired of pandering to your colossal ego. I don't work for you and we both know that."

Dominic growled and flew at Jake, landing a hit that sent Jake back a few feet. "And I'm tired of you talking to me like I wouldn't have a company without you."

Rubbing his quickly-swelling jaw, Jake shoved Dominic backward, toppling the serving table beneath his weight. "You wouldn't."

The fists flew faster, leaving no time for words. It only slowed when both men's faces were swollen and they were holding their sides.

Dominic wiped blood from the corner of his mouth, and actually laughed. "I had no idea you had it in you."

Jake bent over, hands on his thighs, his breathing a bit labored from pain. "It felt surprisingly good."

Mrs. Duhamel made a *tsk* sound with her mouth and said, "Are you boys through, now?"

Dominic looked at the older woman with a bit of chagrin. "You know he had that coming, Marie."

Marie nodded. "I know." To Jake, she said, "You did."

Jake conceded with one nod. "So did he."

Marie smiled. "No one is questioning that, Jake. But now you two need to make up so our poor Abby can enjoy her engagement party."

As usual, she was right.

Jake held out a hand. "Truce?"

Dominic shook it but added, "You're still marrying Lil."

Abby stepped forward at that. "What did you say,

Dom?"

Dominic said, "He heard me."

Abby clarified her question. "I heard you, too, but why would you say that?"

Dominic returned to his place at the head of the table and said unhappily, "Our plan to get the two of them together worked a bit too well."

Abby looked quickly at the door her sister had departed through and exclaimed, "That's why she's so confused this weekend."

Nicole added, "Poor thing."

Dominic placed his napkin decisively on his lap as if doing so would bring an end to the conversation. "Don't worry, Jake is going to rectify the situation."

Abby stood behind Dominic's chair and put a hand on one of his shoulders. "Don't make things worse, Dom."

He scowled up at her.

She touched his cheek lightly and his expression softened. She said, "You can't force Jake. No one wants to marry a man who doesn't want to marry her."

Jake returned to his own place at the table and said, "I never said I didn't want to marry her."

All eyes turned to him.

Jake shrugged. "Well, I didn't."

Stephan's aunt, Elise, said, "Isn't it amazing that men and women get together at all?"

Jake continued, "I even asked her to move in with me, but she said no. Now she won't even talk to me."

Abby said, "I'll go find her." She wagged a finger at

Dominic. "Behave while I'm gone."

He simply smiled up at her and she hesitated.

Stephan's mother, Katrine, said, "Go on, Abby. We've got this." She turned to her sister-in-law. "Elise, doesn't this bring back memories?"

Her husband, Victor, laughed and asked, "Were we this bad?"

Elise threw both hands in the air and joked, "Worse."

Stephan sighed and said, "Makes me almost wish I had a brother." When both Dominic and Jake aggressively jumped to their feet, he quickly dissolved the tension by raising his two hands in an amused call for peace. "Almost."

They sat somewhat reluctantly.

Nicole said, "Zhang left the table, too. Do you think we upset her?"

Katrine said wryly, "I don't know what she could have seen that would make a sane person reconsider having dinner with us."

Nicole smiled and laid her hand on her fiancé's. "At least we know the wedding won't be boring."

Dominic looked across the table at Jake and asked, "Best man?"

Jake dabbed a napkin into his glass of water and pressed it to a cut on his cheek. "Absolutely."

LIL SLIPPED OUT a side door and onto a balcony that overlooked one of the main gardens. To her surprise, it was already occupied. "I'm sorry," she said hastily. "I just couldn't stay in there a moment more."

"Nor could I," Zhang answered.

Lil moved to leave and Zhang said, "Your sister is a wonderful woman. I now proudly count her as one of my friends."

Lil heard something in the woman's voice that gave her pause. She turned and walked back to where Zhang was seated on a bench. "But you don't want to be in her bridal party."

"Precisely." Zhang motioned for Lil to join her. "Is there a customary way to decline the honor without either side losing face?"

Lil sat on the bench beside her. "If you hear of one, tell me. I don't want to be in it either."

A look of surprise crossed over the woman's face, just a brief flash before she regained her composure. "That's surprising."

Lil shook her head sadly. "Not really. If Abby is smart she'll choose someone better suited. I'm a walking disaster."

"That's not the way Abby described you."

"Really?" Lil heard the hope in her voice and was somewhat embarrassed by it.

Zhang's tone warmed. "Abby and I have spoken about you on several occasions. She said you were born with your mother's spirit—quite the warrior soul. She admires your strength."

"I didn't know there was a thing about me that she approved of," Lil said, surprised and moved by Zhang's words.

Zhang didn't let Lil's side comment slide by without rebuttal. "Then you don't know your sister very well. She also envies your circle of friends. She said you collect people who would do anything for you."

"I've always been very lucky with that."

"Friendship is not a result of luck, it's a testament to our character. You inspire loyalty in your friends because you've earned it."

"I don't know how."

Zhang considered her and said, "An eagle will never swim as well as a dolphin. The eagle's potential will only be realized when it decides to soar instead of dive."

Lil cocked her head thoughtfully. "You think I'm trying to be Abby?"

"You tell me."

Lil thought about how she'd always wished she were more like Abby. How, even at their parents' funeral, Abby had seemed able to make better decisions. She hadn't cried too long at the caskets, hadn't refused to meet relatives who had flown in from around the country and definitely hadn't thrown a bowl of candies at someone who had dared to try to console her.

No, right from the start Abby had been the better person.

Or, at the very least, the less controversial one.

Oh, my God, I've been trying to be Abby.

And hating her because I couldn't be.

"Did Abby really say I was like my mother?"

Zhang smiled. "She did. Did you know that your mother was arrested for participating in a war protest?"

Lil's jaw dropped open. "No. I've never heard that story."

"Apparently your mother's fighting heart got her into a few tricky situations—some even involving the law."

That's not possible.

"I don't remember my mother being anything but warm and loving."

"Your sister has been going through some of your parents' old papers and was equally surprised by some of what she found. I'm sure she would love to show you the newspaper clippings if you were interested."

"I am. I can't believe my mother was ever arrested. She was so . . . perfect."

Zhang gave a rueful smile. "The heart remembers people kindly, but no one is perfect. I've heard about some of your adventures and I admire your spirit. You stand up for those you care about. You say what you think, no matter the cost. Those are qualities I respect. You should, too." The simplicity and power of Zhang's comment hung in the reflective quiet that followed them.

Ok, so I'll never be Abby, but if Zhang was right—maybe I don't have to be.

"I've wasted a lot of time second-guessing myself," Lil said, marveling at how comfortable she felt sharing her greatest concern with someone she didn't know. Or perhaps it was simply because she didn't know Zhang that she could say what she had tried to conceal from even herself.

Zhang shrugged. "I didn't get where I am today by never making a mistake."

Maybe I'll be a good mother after all and this year will simply be newspaper clipping my kids will laugh about. "Thank you, Zhang. I can't tell you how much you've helped me."

Zhang nodded, still looking far too solemn.

Her unhappiness was none of Lil's business.

This was exactly the type of crossroad Lil felt she often made the wrong decision at.

Things would go much smoother if she didn't get involved.

I've never really been the one to take the easy road, maybe it's time to embrace that about myself.

"Why don't you want to be in the wedding?" Lil asked.

The same woman who had freely discussed Lil's personal life did not seem as willing to reveal anything about her own. "I'm not exactly the American wedding type."

"You don't want to drink too much while dressed from head-to-toe in mauve taffeta and wake up the next morning wondering why you French kissed your best friend's brother?"

Zhang didn't so much as crack a smile.

Tough crowd.

"Something like that," Zhang said.

"Why do I get the feeling you've never done that?"

That did get Zhang to smile.

"I haven't either." At Zhang's raised eyebrow, Lil admitted, "Okay, once . . . maybe twice."

Zhang shook her head in amusement.

Lil defended herself with humor. "Hey, don't knock it until you've tried it. Something about weddings makes me a little nutty."

The other woman's smile slipped away. "Weddings make

me sad."

Now, we're getting somewhere.

"Is that the reason you don't want to be in Abby's?"

Zhang didn't respond for a moment. Instead, she took in the night sky as if no response were anticipated. Finally, she said, "I'm the woman I wanted to become. I have more than I could have ever imagined. I've done more than I ever dreamt I could. But I'm alone."

It was difficult for Lil to imagine that a woman as confident and beautiful as Zhang wouldn't have a man in her life. The real sadness in her voice hinted at a level of loneliness more profound than a romantic dry spell.

"Don't you have a family?" Lil asked.

"Yes, of course. My parents often join me in whichever home I am using at the time, but I go to sleep alone. I wake up alone. When I close on a deal and want to celebrate I can call friends who wonder how much money will be enough for me, parents who think it's time for me to concentrate on finding a husband, or keep the news to myself. I often choose the latter." Zhang's intense black eyes revealed a pain Lil was certain the woman had not shared with many. "Your sister tells me that you won't accept anyone's help because you want to be independent. Be careful what you wish for. Sometimes it's not everything you thought it would be."

Lil thought about Jake. She'd been afraid that she would lose herself if she accepted any help from him but, looking back, Jake had consistently shown her that he valued her interests and her goals. It would have been easy for a man of his wealth to dismiss her desire to finish her degree, but he hadn't. Another man might have asked to see one of her sketches and buried her beneath a deluge of flattery that would have meant nothing, but Jake hadn't done that either. He had respected the desire every artist has to learn and improve. Her gut told her that Jake wouldn't make her choose—she could still be a strong, independent woman and be his.

If only he loved her.

Yes, he wanted her. Yes, he respected her, but what if he had nothing more than that to offer her?

Even if I take my betrayal with me to the grave . . . is half of Jake better than none?

There were plenty of things Lil had no control over: she couldn't make Jake love her, she couldn't undo the past, but she could damn well put her insecurities aside and do the right thing for Abby.

"I'll make you a deal, Zhang."

The woman looked at her.

"I'll find Abby and tell her that I'd love to be her maid of honor if you say yes to being a bridesmaid. You keep me out of trouble at the wedding and I'll make you laugh."

Zhang's expression was difficult to interpret.

"Deal?" Lil asked hopefully.

"Yes," she said slowly.

Abby stepped out onto the balcony. "Oh, this is where you two disappeared to."

Zhang stood and said, "Excuse me, but I know the two of you have things you need to discuss."

Lil touched Zhang's arm before she left and said, "Thank

you."

Zhang nodded with a smile that reached her eyes and said, "Don't be afraid to soar, Lil. Find your wings." Then she exited the balcony.

ABBY CAME TO sit beside her sister. At first neither said anything and then they both said, "I'm sorry," in union and stopped.

Lil said, "I wish life had a do-over button, Abby. I feel like I have so much to apologize to you for."

Abby took her sister's hand in one of hers. "I understand that feeling all too well."

Lil squeezed her hand. "I blamed you for so many things that were not your fault, Abby."

Abby put a supportive arm around her. "Oh, don't worry, some of it was my fault, I'm sure. I wanted to be there for you, Lil, so much so that sometimes I didn't listen to what you were telling me you needed."

Lil said, "I'm sorry that I embarrassed you in front of the Andrade family."

Abby gave her a small smile. "Trust me, your walk out was not the most embarrassing part of the meal."

Lil shook her head in confusion. "Really? What happened after I left?"

Abby suggested, "Let's talk about that later. First, I want to apologize for putting you in an awkward position by asking you to be my maid of honor with an audience."

Lil could not have felt worse than she did. She met her sister's eyes and hoped the extent of her remorse showed in her expression. "Well, I'm sure you thought, rightfully so, that my answer would be a yes."

Abby touched her sister's cheek softly as a mother would touch a child they weren't sure how to console. "Either way, it was wrong, and I respect your decision. I don't understand it, but I know that you didn't say it to hurt me."

"I'm scared," Lil blurted.

"Of what, Lil?" Abby asked in surprise.

It was time for honesty, at least, for as much as she could share without endangering her friends. "What if I do something that takes all of this away from you? You're finally happy. I love seeing you with Dominic, but I feel like the closer I come to you and your wedding—the more potential there is that I could mess something up."

Abby hugged Lil closer and said, "If my relationship with Dominic is so fragile that it can't survive a Lil Dartley escapade, then it wasn't going to last anyway."

Lil pulled back and searched her sister's face. "How can you be like that? How can you look the worst case in the eye without being afraid?"

Abby smiled sadly and confessed, "Who said I'm not afraid? I'm flipping terrified half the time and I have been since Mom and Dad died."

"Really?" That didn't sound like Abby.

"Lil, I was eighteen when they passed away. I had no idea how to pay bills, keep a house, mother someone."

The enormity of the responsibility that had fallen onto Abby's shoulders at an age when she should have been thinking only of herself filled Lil with sudden shame. What could she say to someone who had given up so much and been shown so little respect in return? How do you begin to make up for that? "But you did it."

"Yes, and I still go to sleep each night wondering if I've done any of it well."

"You have, Abby. You have nothing to regret."

Unlike me.

"Lil, fear is a nasty little condition that touches everyone's life at one time or another. Dominic may look all tough on the outside, but he gets scared just like you and I do. He has a box of his father's papers, one that was sent back to him from the auction Nicole had, and he won't open it. There could be bonds, deeds, or a personal letter from his father, but he says he doesn't want to know what's in it. He says he's spent too many unhappy years to risk losing what he has now over something in that box of papers. Imagine worrying that whatever is in there could ruin his new relationship with his sister and possibly even what we have. Fear is a disease that no one is immune to."

Lil had no idea what to say. She sat quietly absorbing her sister's words.

Abby said, "Jake is no better. I used to think he had it all together, but I've watched him try to handle this China situation and he is coming undone over it."

"The China situation?"

Abby hesitated then said, "I probably shouldn't even talk to you about it, but the server Dominic was supposed to put online next month has been hacked and corrupted. We could lose everything if the deal goes south. That's one reason we want to have the wedding early—we don't know what life will be like a month from now."

Oh, my God! That brought a whole new meaning to for richer or poorer.

"Abby, I had no idea!"

"No one does. Well, we're hoping no one does. I'm only telling you this because it might explain why Jake may not be showing you his best right now. He's under an extreme amount of pressure to help Dominic find a solution and so far nothing has worked."

So, that explained why he was flying all over the country and paying hush money.

Could Jeremy have found something that could help them?

Abby said, "This weekend doubles as an engagement party and a cover for Dominic to fly in some big named programmers without sending up any red flags. Jake is going to need a friend, Lil, especially at the party tomorrow."

Ok, now you've lost me.

"I don't understand."

Abby said, "Dominic is counting on enlisting the help of two of the biggest icons in computer programming history."

Lil shrugged.

Still nothing.

Abby said with emphasis, "Jake's parents."

"And that's a bad thing?" Even as she voiced the question, Lil thought back to when she'd asked Jake about his parents and how he'd become defensive.

"Dominic told me that Jake has never even admitted that

they are his parents. He refuses to talk about them at all."

I believe that.

"Then how did Dominic get them to come?" When it came to her future brother-in-law the possibilities were endless.

"He told them that Jake wanted them here."

"Oh, that's not good." Jake was not going to be happy with that lie.

"Dom is convinced it will work out." Abby didn't look as certain. She gripped Lil's hand as something occurred to her. "You can't tell Jake, Lil."

"I won't."

"I shouldn't have said anything."

Lil gave her sister's hand a supportive squeeze. "I won't say a word."

And she meant it.

Unfortunately, I'm becoming quite good at lying by omission.

Time to change the subject. "Abby, I'll be your maid of honor."

With a happy gasp, Abby hugged her long and tight. "I am so happy, Lil."

Lil hugged her back and wished she could say the same. "I do have a request, though."

"Oh, oh," Abby said with an indulgent smile.

"Choose dresses for the wedding party that are smoking hot. I mean eat-your-heart-out-and-wish-you-could-have-a-piece-of-this, but sophisticated," Lil said.

Abby laughed. "I'll tell Marie. She is fantastic with stuff

like that."

"You get along with her really well, don't you?" Lil asked.

Abby said, "I know Dominic has a mother, but Marie is the one he turns to when he needs a mom."

Lil coughed, "Dominic needs a mom?"

Abby smiled. "Everyone needs someone in their life who loves them unconditionally and will still remind them to watch their manners."

Lil shook her head in wonder. "Somehow I can't picture anyone telling Dominic to do that."

Abby threw a hand up for emphasis and laughed. "Oh, it's hilarious to see. She puts Jake in his place now and then, too."

Now that I would like to see.

"Isn't she just Dominic's assistant?" Lil asked.

"That's what she'll try to tell you, but she's so much more. She came into their lives about seven years ago. Dominic had just taken over the Andrade's family company and was in a huge fight with his sister. Jake disagreed with how Dom was handling the situation to the point where he had threatened to pull out of the company. From what I understand, Marie witnessed one of those escalating arguments and told them that she was mortified by their behavior. Dominic does the funniest impression of Marie— you'll have to ask to hear it one day. *Stop bickering this instant. You sound like two young schoolgirls. Jake, can't you see that Dominic is hurt over what is happening with his sister? Support him a little. And, Dominic, you apologize right now for threatening to kill Jake. And watch your language. In my day, men didn't use profanity in front of women so I'd appreciate it if you both refrained from being quite so graphic in the future.* Dom told me that when they both stopped laughing they actually did as she suggested. He and Jake were friends since college, but Marie made them a family."

Wow.

"What about Dominic's mother? Rosella?" It had to be hard for her to watch another woman assume her role in her child's life. Lil couldn't imagine how she would feel if something like that ever happened with her and Colby. Just the idea of it was heartbreaking.

Abby said, "Dominic has seen her several times. He loves her, but it's still strained. Maybe it always will be. She hurt her children by leaving them. Hurt like that doesn't just go away."

"Was that who Nicole was referring to when she said that someone could come tomorrow?" *Ah, it made sense now.*

"Yes, and that was a huge step for her. Outside of one quick meeting, Nicole has refused to see her."

"I can't really blame her. She thought her mother was dead." Lil found it difficult to find any sympathy for a woman who had deserted her children and faked her own death to protect herself.

Abby said, "We're only on this planet for so long, Lil. Life is too short and too precious to nurture old injuries. Sometimes it's better to just let it go so you can heal."

Oh, really? This claim needed to be tested.

"That means you've completely forgiven me for totaling

your first car?"

A slight red filled Abby's cheeks. "The one I had finally paid off and could have driven for free for years if you hadn't taken it for a joyride before you had your driver's license?"

Perhaps that had been the wrong injury to resurrect. "When you say it like that, it does sound awful."

Abby patted one of Lil's shoulders in mock support. "I've forgiven you, but that doesn't mean I won't enjoy watching Colby put you through your paces."

"That hurts," Lil laughed.

"The truth often does," Abby joked back.

Lil sobered and asked, "We're okay, right, Abby?"

Abby hugged her sister one last time and used a line that she'd started saying when she'd taken over the household and had continued to sprinkle into many of their disagreements over the years. "Always better together."

Tears welled and spilled down Lil's cheeks. Oh, how she'd mocked Abby over the years for voicing that mantra whenever things had gotten dicey between them. Today, she finally heard something in those words that she'd thought Abby had never said. It made her feel both ashamed of how she'd taken her sister for granted and grateful that somehow Abby had loved her through it all.

For the first time, Lil repeated the words in agreement, "Always better together."

Her normally composed sister hugged her tighter and burst into tears.

Happy tears.

Cleansing tears.

"About that car," Lil added to lighten the mood.

Abby pulled back slightly and smiled even as she wiped her wet cheeks. "Still going to enjoy your pain."

"I love you, too, Abby." Lil meant to say the words with some sarcasm, but they came out as a heartfelt declaration.

Abby's smile widened and she stood, offering a hand to her sister. "I know, Lil. Now, let's go pick out which dress you're going to wear for the big party tomorrow night. We'll see if we have the same definition of smoking hot."

LATER THAT NIGHT Lil was choosing a book to read to Colby. She picked up and dismissed each from the selection she had packed. Finally, she settled Colby onto her lap with only a bottle and said, "From now on we're going to read alphabet books instead of this junk. None of these books prepare you for real life. It's never as easy as having the right sized foot, men do not fall in love with you because they hear you sing one song, and if seven men ever ask you to move in with them—I want you to say no."

Colby was more interested in her evening meal than her mother's impromptu life lesson.

"All sound advice," Jake said from behind her.

Lil whipped around in her seat, hearing a slight protest from Colby before she settled back with her bottle again. "What are you doing here?"

"We need to talk."

"This is my private suite. You can't just come in here."

"Do you want me to go out and knock again? You didn't answer last time."

"Oh, I'm sorry. I didn't hear you." Then she thought about it. "Wait, I'm not sorry. If no one answers, you don't just walk in."

There was a bit too much *I do as I please* look in his eyes for her comfort. "You had the opportunity to talk to me downstairs."

"Another man would take the hint."

"I'm tired of playing games, Lil. It's time for us to be honest."

Honest.

Maybe he was right. Maybe the only way to get past this was for her to tell him everything. He wasn't a vindictive man. Once she explained to him that Alethea and Jeremy had only been trying to find out if Abby was safe—he'd understand.

And there was a good chance that Jeremy had discovered something useful.

Abby would likely never forgive her if she went that extra step and told Jake that Dominic had invited his parents, but didn't he deserve to know? After all, hadn't Jake spent the last few weeks trying to save Dominic? He didn't deserve to be broadsided like that.

Honesty, here I come.

"Yes, it is," she said. "And I have something I need to tell you . . ." As he stepped away from the doorway and into the room Lil noticed that one of his eyes was blackened as if it had been punched. He crouched beside her chair and she touched a bruise on his jaw. "What happened to your face?"

"Dominic didn't like the truth."

Instant outrage filled Lil. "He beat you up?"

Oddly, Jake looked pleased with himself. "I'd call it more of a tie."

"What were you fighting about?"

There was always a chance it wasn't about her, but she was beginning to think that telling the truth might not be the best idea. So far honesty looked painful.

"A difference of opinion . . ." he said.

"About?"

"Does it matter?"

"It might."

Jake pushed a lock of hair behind her ear. "Dom and I have been friends since college. We built Corisi Enterprises from nothing. I have never minded that he wanted to be the face of the company. However, sometimes he forgets that I've invested as much into it as he has."

"And you punched him to remind him?"

"He swung first." Jake's expression became more intimate. "It seems that someone told him we slept together."

Lil blushed straight down to the roots of her hair. "Yeah, about that . . ."

He smiled and traced her bottom lip with a finger. "You're not a very good secret keeper."

Oh, you'd be surprised.

"Jake . . ."

He put a hand on either side of her chair and said, "It doesn't matter. He would have found out eventually, anyway. And it doesn't change how I feel. I intend to marry you, Lillian Dartley."

The room spun.

Breathe.

Lil looked down at her daughter and said, "Colby, men say that to get what they want."

Jake took Lil's chin in his hand and lifted her face so she had to meet his eyes. "Boys do that, Lil, not men."

He took her lips gently with his in a kiss like none she'd ever experienced. It felt like—a promise.

She pulled back and stood, forcing him to step back. "Colby is tired."

"I'll wait."

A wave of emotions shook her. He'd said the marriage word again, but no mention of love. Had Dominic told him to marry her? She was sure she didn't want to know the answer to that question.

"I'm tired," she said.

Although he seemed to have more to say, Jake nodded, kissed the top of Colby's head softly and stepped back. Lil's heart swelled in her chest. *If it looked like love and acted like love—it could be love, couldn't it?*

"We'll continue this conversation tomorrow." He walked halfway to the door and turned. "What did you want to tell me, Lil? You never said."

Absolutely nothing came to mind.

Lil shrugged awkwardly. "I don't remember."

And, sadly, for just the time it took for him to leave the room fear kept her mind blank.

Reality returned with the click of the door closing behind him.

Colby pinched her mother's chin. Lil looked down and smiled at her impudence. "Really? You think you would have told him? I can't wait until you're in love with someone. You'll see that it's not that easy."

Chapter Thirteen

THE ENGAGEMENT PARTY was held at one of Dominic's immense country estates about thirty minutes from New York City. Lil and Abby had gone over the details with the staff in the morning to ensure that everything went smoothly. Security was evident in every corner of the compound.

Mrs. Duhamel had offered to watch Colby for the day so Lil could support Abby as she fluctuated from being excited about the big day to being a nervous wreck. It still amazed Lil that beneath her strong façade, Abby worried and succumbed to the occasional panic just like she did.

To alleviate their stress, Abby and Lil spent two hours having their hair and nails done by the stylists Dominic had hired for them. Eventually Lil had returned to her own suite to dress alone. Well, alone was really an exaggeration of the situation. Lil was feeling a bit crowded by the entourage whose sole job was to anticipate her every need. Abby said she wouldn't notice the staff or the security after a while, but Lil was longing for the privacy of her penthouse. Did Jake live like this? Lil couldn't imagine him tolerating the constant intrusion.

That evening, Lil stood at the top of the stairs in a sleeveless, floor-length orange dress, wondering if she had chosen her attire wisely. Many of the women she could see were much more demurely dressed in either a sophisticated black or subdued red.

Nicole waved to Lil from across the room, looking every bit as comfortable in her floor-length, off-one-shoulder, claret Erdem dress. She and Stephan move seamlessly through the crowd, stopping to engage in what appeared to be just the right amount of small talk with each group of guests before moving on to the next cluster of people.

Dominic and Abby were located at the far end of the hall, greeting people who were casually making their way to meet them. The party looked like a scene out of a movie. Everyone looked so poised, so perfect.

I don't even know how to address them.

I should have asked.

No, I should have pretended to be sick tonight, that's what I really should have done.

How am I going to be Abby's maid of honor if I'm not even brave enough to leave the top of the stairway?

As if on cue, Jake appeared at the bottom of the stairs in a simple, formal tuxedo. The warmth in his eyes as he looked up at her freed her feet. She forced herself to take the stairs gracefully instead of flying to his side as she wanted to.

When she reached him, he kissed her lightly on the cheek, linked her arm with his and whispered, "You look stunning tonight."

Tucked against his side, lost in the magic of the evening,

she lowered her sarcastic shield and replied, "So, do you."

He stopped and looked down at her, smiling. "Ms. Dartley, did you just give me a compliment?"

She couldn't help but return his smile. "I can be nice."

He bent and growled into her ear, "But I've begun to consider your taunts a form of foreplay."

She playfully swatted his arm. "You would."

His words tickled her ear. "If we were alone I would show you exactly what you do to me, but I can wait until tonight."

"Tonight?" Her throat dried and her heart pounded in her chest.

"Oh, yes, after Dom and Abby make their announcement, I'm going to steal you away to my private suite in the north wing."

"And just what makes you think I'll go with you?"

He ducked behind a potted plant with her and claimed her lips hungrily. She hesitated for just a second before meeting his lips enthusiastically. His tongue teased then entered, coaxing and exciting. His hands molded her frame to his, firmly holding her against the evidence of his need for her. "You'll come."

He set her back from him and adjusted her clothing.

I'm sure I will, she thought and fanned her face. *Maybe more than once.*

"I love that expression on your face," he said.

She cocked her head in question.

They stepped out from behind the plant and he said, "The one that says that you have a naughty thought that you're not going to share. I'll spend the entire evening wondering exactly what you were thinking just then."

"I could tell you," she said boldly.

He pulled her into his side as they walked and growled suggestively, "Why not simply show me later?"

She would have said something witty if she had been able to think coherently. Much more of this and she was going to suggest they cut the evening short and consequences be damned. Instead she gathered her resolve and regained some clarity by focusing on the people around them. Jake escorted her through the crowd and introduced her to everyone from a prime minister to a sheikh. He didn't introduce her with a label, but his arm never left her waist and the message that she was his could not have been more obvious if he had rented a billboard.

Not that Lil minded.

His possessiveness gave her another reason to hope.

Lil was allowing herself to relax and enjoy the evening when she saw someone across the room who immediately changed her mood.

Jake felt her tense and asked, "Is there something wrong?"

Oh, just potentially, everything.

"No," Lil answered evasively. "I just saw a friend of mine."

Jake scanned the room and asked coldly, "Who?"

His tone made her temporarily return her focus to him. "Are you jealous?"

"No," he said in an angry tone. "No," he said again,

sounding like he was aiming for a more casual answer. Then he turned her more fully toward him. "Should I be?"

No, but if you knew everything you might wish this were about another man.

"Not unless you think my taste is tall, red-haired women."

He let out a slow breath. "Your friend Alethea?"

Her eyebrows furrowed, "How do you know about her?" Then she remembered. "Would you stop reading my background check, please? It's not fair."

"Is it my fault they were so thorough?"

"It's going to be your fault if I stomp this heel into your toes."

He nodded. "Point made."

Lil tried to pull away. "Excuse me, I have to go speak to her for a moment . . ."

"I'll go with you."

"No, you can't because . . ." She stopped herself. *No more lies.* "Jake, do you trust me?"

His expression was unreadable. Then he said, "Yes."

"Believe me when I tell you I have to talk to Alethea alone and I can't tell you why. I want to tell you, but it doesn't involve just me." She took his hand in hers, trying to convey the importance without giving anything away.

"That sounds pretty ominous."

"It might end up being something good, but I can't say more than that right now. Can you do that for me? Can you give me a little time to figure this out?"

He looked like that was the last thing he wanted to do,

but he said, "Trust goes both ways, Lil."

"I know," Lil said huskily. *I hope I don't lose yours over this.*

"I'll go get us a drink," he said and withdrew his arm from around her.

No, she wanted to cry, but she let him walk away. Somehow, she was going to make this right.

She flew to Alethea's side and grabbed her arm. "What the hell are you doing here?" Lil hissed at her friend.

"You're not going to congratulate me for successfully gaining entry to one of the most heavily guarded events in recent history? I even snuck Jeremy in. He's at the appetizer table."

Lil looked over and saw a man eating everyone's share of the shrimp. *Oh, my God.* "I thought we agreed you weren't going to do this."

Alethea flipped her thick crimson hair over one bare shoulder. In a simple, black, floor-length Tom Ford gown, Alethea blended well with the crowd, looking more like a movie star that night than a security consultant. Her eyes flashed with annoyance. "You should have told me the Waltons were coming. They are like the holy grail of computer programmers. No one was even sure they were still alive until word came that they were coming to this event. I couldn't miss it. Hell, Jeremy shaved and left his basement to meet them. They are that big."

"You're not worried about exposing everything by bringing him here?"

"No, because Jeremy has assured me that no one will ever

know what we did unless we say something about it." Alethea gave her friend a meaningful look. "And we're not going to, are we, Lil?"

Lil's composure cracked. Her feelings gushed out. "I have to tell them, Al. Jake and Dominic are in real jeopardy of losing their company if they don't fix their server issue and Jeremy might be the only one who knows something that could help them."

"I was afraid you were going to say that," Alethea sighed. "You've never been a good liar."

Lil brought a grateful and shaky hand to her mouth as she realized her friend's true motive for being there that night. "You brought Jeremy in case I need him."

Alethea nodded and said, "I also know of at least three ways out of here if this goes south."

Lil looked across at the man who was stashing crab cakes in the pockets of his checkered dinner jacket. "And Jeremy is onboard with this? He'll help us?"

Alethea grimaced and said, "He really does want to meet the Waltons, but I may have also promised to run away with him to Mexico if Dominic decides to press charges and we have to escape and create new identities for ourselves."

Lil bit her lip to stop from finding amusement in a situation that was really too scary to warrant it. "He likes you that much, huh?"

Alethea shuddered. "Yeah, make sure it doesn't come to that. He's not my type." She looked around the room and nodded in the direction of a well-built, intense-looking man who was dressed in a tuxedo but was far too alert to be one of the guests. "Now that man could frisk me, any day."

As always, Alethea's choice was one of the most dangerous men in the room. "That's Dominic's head of security. He does not have a sense of humor." She tried to regain her friend's attention by elbowing her discreetly. "Stop making eyes at him. If he finds out you snuck in here we're both dead."

"Don't worry about Mr. Sour Grapes; I can handle him." Alethea winked at the man across the room and smiled when the act brought a rush of angry color to his face. "Oh, yeah. I might actually have some fun."

"No, Al, no fun," Lil pleaded. "Promise me you'll play it cool tonight. We'll be lucky enough if we don't land ourselves in jail when this is all over."

Alethea sighed dramatically. "Fine, killjoy. The sacrifices we make for friendship . . ."

Asking her to stay out of trouble was like asking your dog to stay off the couch. Sure both might look innocent enough while you were right there with them, but you had a pretty good idea about how things would go down as soon as you left.

"It would serve you right to spend the rest of your life as Mrs. Jeremy Kater or whatever new name you two lovebirds came up with."

"Nice, Lil. I'll remember that when the police cars pull up."

Lil sobered for a moment as the real possibility of that thing happening settled on her and she realized the enormity of what her friend was willing to risk for her. "They won't when Jeremy tells Jake what he found. Thank you, Al."

Alethea shrugged off Lil's gratitude, but Lil knew it had touched her friend to hear it. "Go—" Alethea said. "Go get Jeremy and save your man. I'll be here if you need me."

With one last grateful hug, Lil left her friend's side to do just that.

Chapter Fourteen

TAKING ADVANTAGE OF Lil's momentary absence, Jake shouldered up to Dominic. "So where is this couple you think has the answer to all of our problems?"

Dominic hesitated, a sure sign that he was up to something he didn't think Jake would approve of. "Victor is entertaining them in the study. They aren't too keen on being seen in public."

"But they were willing to come to an event like this?"

Dominic shrugged. "You were enough of a lure."

"Who the hell . . ." As soon as the idea came to him, he tensed with growing anger. "Tell me you didn't bring my parents here."

"Are your parents named James and Judith Walton?"

"Dominic!" Jake rubbed a hand over his eyes. "You just wasted another week of our time on a dead end. They haven't worked in the computer field for almost ten years."

"They seemed to understand what our issue is."

"That's because they are geniuses, but a decade of farming in Maine is not good preparation for something like this."

"It's amazing to think that they went from two of the most renowned physicists who to practically invented quantum encryption—to absolute obscurity. Didn't they accuse the government of stealing their software designs for the military?"

"Yes, they did. They claimed that some of their experiments with laser beams were stolen and used to advance the guided missile program. They are also convinced that Ivan Getting stole their initial Global Positioning notes and sold them to the military."

"You don't believe them?"

Jake shot a glare at Dominic. "I stopped caring what the truth was a long time ago. My parents have paid a high price for the gift of intelligence. They built a shared reality based on paranoia and an over-inflated sense of self-importance. I'm surprised you got them to leave their compound at all."

Dominic shrugged. "They said they missed you. How long has it been since you've seen them?"

"Are you honestly going to lecture me about family relationships?" He shook his head at the irony overload. "I don't have a vendetta against my parents; I simply don't have a close relationship with them. In fact, I find that the less time I spend with them, the happier we all are."

"They didn't seem that bad to me."

"You didn't grow up with them," Jake growled.

Dominic smiled. "Are you getting angry about this?"

"No," Jake gritted his teeth as even he heard the emotion in his denial. He took a calming breath. "Don't be surprised if they refuse to help. If it doesn't have to do with something they are working on—or apparently planting lately—they don't usually spare any time for it."

"They cared enough to come here, Jake. Give them that much credit."

A bit too late for them to pretend to be doting parents. When Jim and Judy were together, they didn't need anyone else—they never had. Why they'd bothered to have Jake at all still baffled him. He had been a responsibility that came after science, after each other, and after their growing distrust of the government. More times than he cared to remember they'd forgotten to pick him up from school, to make meals for him, to check that he had clean clothes. He'd learned early that the only one he could rely on was himself. At the age of eleven, he'd chosen a boarding school and enrolled himself. A small part of him had hoped that they would wake up and beg him not to go, but instead they had lauded his choice of schools and deposited him there with a disgusting amount of relief.

He'd found reasons why he couldn't go home each summer—internships, study abroad programs. The reason didn't matter to his parents, nor did his destination. They sent money when he asked for it and, he supposed, that was all that mattered in the end.

Holidays had always been the worst. In the beginning he'd had a choice between going home to parents who didn't believe in celebrating days that they claimed governments or religions had arbitrarily chosen to give importance to, going home with a friend with a close-knit family who only reminded him painfully of what he didn't have, or spending the holiday alone.

Meeting Dominic in college had offered a much better alternative . . . designing a company that would grow and one day dominate the computer market.

He never felt sorry for himself when he was adding another figure to his income bracket.

They say that money can't make you happy, but it had made his life a whole lot more bearable. Until quite recently he would have said there wasn't a single thing he would change about his life.

Now there was only one.

He wanted Lil in it. Lil and Colby.

He didn't want to wake up Monday morning in his house if neither of them were there. He wouldn't have to, though, because he'd already decided that they would be coming home with him at the end of the weekend. Lil would accept his proposal once she thought it through.

She'd have to wait, though. His parents were the more pressing matter at hand. "I'll talk to them, Dom, but get ready to aggressively begin the search for help again on Monday."

JAKE BRACED HIMSELF and opened the door to the study, "Judy. Jim. What a pleasant surprise."

His mother broke her conversation with her husband and Victor Andrade when she heard her son's voice. At first glance, she looked much the same as she always had; except perhaps that her dark, shoulder-length hair sported a bit more gray. Her signature cream knit sweater and tan loose trousers were expensive, yet understated and unadorned with jewelry. Although both of his parents had been born into wealthy families, neither had ever looked the part; preferring to spend their money on their research rather than any of the earthly possessions most people collected. His father's gray hair was too long for the style he'd attempted to brush it into, indicating that he'd probably forgotten his last trim appointment. He was dressed in the same dark blue dinner jacket and purple, striped tie that he'd likely worn to every formal event in the past twenty years. Not much had changed in the three years since Jake had last seen them.

"Jake," his mother said in greeting. She didn't walk over to give him a hug.

He hadn't expected her to, so really there was no reason for the twinge of disappointment he felt. In about thirty seconds, his parents could do what no one else could; they could make him feel insignificant. He joined the group and shook the hand his father offered.

His father studied his face for a moment then asked, "Are you okay, Jake?"

Jake touched one of the bruises on his cheek and said, "It looks worse than it is."

Victor slapped Jake on the back and laughed, "And better than the other guy, *si*?"

Jake smiled before meeting his mother's look of disapproval. Even though she said nothing, he could hear her voice in his head. *We do not condone physical violence, Jake.*

He sighed.

His mother said, "Victor has been filling us in on what

has been going on. I'm surprised that your company was using such a weak symmetric key encryption algorithm for your access codes."

Jake defended their practice. "Yes, many of our protocols use symmetric encryption, but our more sensitive data transfers utilize an asymmetric, hybrid cipher. It's perfectly acceptable to use the more secure to initiate access and not to relay the bulk of the data."

"You wouldn't be in this situation today if you had used quantum keys," his mother chided.

"Your mother is right, Jake," his father concurred.

"That wasn't my decision. I am not a programmer."

His mother interrupted him, "You should be. You're wasting your talent. You are far too intelligent to be Dominic Corisi's lackey."

Every muscle in his body tensed and his reaction could not be contained. "I am a multi-billionaire. I employ hundreds of thousands of people all across the globe. Countries have entered the technological race because of the advances I've helped bring to them. I'm sorry if I don't want to sit in a lab somewhere, tinkering with protons until I invent the perfect encryption key or, having given up on that, take up farming in some New England redneck town. I'm not you."

"Show your parents the respect they deserve, Jake," Victor said in a stern tone.

"That's exactly what I'm doing," Jake snarled.

Victor started to say something else, but Judy stopped him with a placating wave of her hand. "No, Victor, he's right. I didn't mean to belittle your accomplishments, Jake. Of course we're proud that you're rich. We just hoped for so much more from you."

The verbal pat on the head did not lessen Jake's temper, but Jake resolved to. He took a deep, calming breath. His parents would never see the value of what he did. It shouldn't bother him. Inviting them this weekend had been a profound waste of time and he was about to prove it. "We have just over three weeks until our server goes online in China. Do you think you and Jim can find the cause of the compromised codes?"

His father answered, "We won't know for sure until we're given access to the program, but it sounds like there is something else going on. Some of your patches seemed to work initially and then were corrupted? That hints at either a Trojan virus or some back door access code. If your original hacker was good enough, those codes can be difficult to locate. Not impossible, but the process might be time consuming. There is no way to say if we'll meet your deadline. It'd be a whole lot easier if we knew what we were dealing with."

"Just say you can't do it," Jake goaded.

Judy Walton walked over to her son and raised a hand to touch her son's cheek, but Jake pulled his head away from her touch. She let her hand drop to her side. "We want to help you."

Jake ran a hand through his normally pristine hair, "But you've been out of the field for a long time, I know. Dominic should never have asked you."

Jim joined his wife, putting an arm lightly around her waist in quiet support. "Do you know what we're working on, Jake?"

"Farming techniques?" Jake said dismissively.

His father shook his head. "Far from it." He looked over at Victor as if assessing if he could be trusted with certain information. He said, "We're bio-engineering the next generation of encryption—organic keys—encoding information at the DNA level. Imagine having chemical access codes stored within your very own cells. Codes that remain intact even as the strands change as a result of breeding. Technology could truly be something you leave your children."

Victor waved an excited hand in the air and said, "That's impossible. You can't add codes to DNA without changing their function."

Jim countered with a humble shrug. "It's impossible in animals so far, but we've proven it can work with certain plants."

DNA encryption? His parents were wandering further from reality than he'd thought. "Another world-changing discovery? Aren't you afraid Victor will steal the idea now that you've shared it?"

His mother looked over her shoulder at her husband and then back at her son. The lines of her face deepened with emotion. "Your father and I have come to an awful realization recently—we're not going to be here forever. We've spent some time re-evaluating our priorities."

Jake sighed impatiently and half-turned away from her.

"Judy, don't take this as harshly as it sounds, but I don't have time to entertain your mid-life crisis right now."

His father nodded, but his tone was surprisingly firm. "We probably deserve that comment, Son, but give your mother a few more minutes of your time."

It was really only Victor's presence that held Jake's tongue. "Fine. I'm listening."

His mother looked uncomfortable—almost nervous—as she said, "I know we weren't the parents you wanted, Jake. You wanted someone to rush to school when you scraped a knee or cook for some bake sale."

Not about to sugarcoat the past, Jake said, "I would have been happy if you had just attended one of my graduations."

"It's not an excuse, Jake, but research can be addictive. You get so close to a breakthrough—you don't want to walk away. Time escapes you and suddenly you realize another day has gone by."

"Well, then I suppose I should thank you for coming here at all," Jake said unkindly.

To his surprise, his mother clasped her hands in front of her as if she found his words upsetting. "Your father and I made some mistakes. We didn't protect ourselves or our discoveries as well as we should have and because of that we lost some of them to others. But do you know what we regret more than any of that?"

Jake shook his head and glanced at his watch.

"We didn't protect you from our obsession." Her voice shook and Jake felt an anger burning in his stomach. He didn't want her words to touch him, to reawaken a yearning he'd put behind him years ago. "We missed your childhood and I know that you'd rather be anywhere but here with us, but don't shut us out. We love you."

"Love?" Jake recoiled from the word. "Love is for people who have nothing better to believe in. I don't need love. I need to know if you can fix the server and then disappear back to that northern farm you think you'll change the world from."

A gasp from the doorway echoed through the painful silence that had followed Jake's harsh words.

"Lil!" he said and took a few steps toward her.

She held up a hand to stop his advance. "No, don't say anything else. I had almost convinced myself that you actually cared about me and Colby, but now I see that you're not capable of caring for anyone, are you?"

A man who appeared to be in his mid-twenties, dressed in a brown checkered dinner jacket that didn't look like it quite fit him—too long at the sleeves a bit loose around the waist. With zero dress sense and even less survival skills, the man chose that moment to walk over to Jake's parents and say, "Hey, aren't you the Waltons? This is so cool."

Jake grabbed one of Lil's arms as she was turning to leave. "You misunderstood what you heard."

She gave her arm a yank, but he didn't let it go. "Oh, I understood perfectly. You really mean all that trash you say."

"This was not about you." Regardless of what happened between him and Lil, chances were good that she would never see his parents again, anyway.

Lil shook her head violently. "I disagree. I feel sorry for

whatever happened to you that left a black hole where your heart should be, but I can't be with a man who thinks love is something you outgrow believing in like Santa Claus."

"Don't do this, Lil," he warned.

His tone seemed to enrage her. Instead of pulling away, she went nose to nose with him and spat, "Don't do what? Don't expect better from you? Get your hand off of me."

Jake didn't. He couldn't. He had to make her see. "You're making a big deal out of nothing."

His words didn't have the soothing effect he'd hoped for.

"That's because I just realized that what we have is exactly that . . . nothing." She closed her eyes as if the thought hurt her. "I can't believe I was willing to put my friends in jeopardy for you. I'm such an idiot."

"What are you talking about?"

Lil opened her eyes, hurt turning to anger. She tore her arm out of Jake's grasp. "Ask Jeremy. But understand that I'm only helping you now for Abby and Dominic's sake."

With that she ran out of the room.

Jake's loyalty was torn. *You can only fix one problem at a time.* He turned his attention to the man who was already deep in conversation with his parents. "Will someone explain to me what the hell is going on?"

Jeremy took a bite out of a crab cake and said, "Man, women will make you nuts, won't they? First I'm asked to hack into your computer like it's no big deal. Then I'm told I could meet two programming icons as long as I take that secret with me to the grave. Now I'm supposed to save your company by spilling what I know about the backdoor I found to your mainframe . . ."

"You found a backdoor access point?"

The young man held up a hand. "Only if it means you're not going to prosecute me for admitting any of this. Not that you could prove it, anyway. I cover my tracks well." He smiled at Jake's mother, looking quite pleased with himself.

Jim interjected, "Knowing what we are dealing with is going to make all the difference. We should be able to have the server debugged in plenty of time now."

The news didn't bring Jake the sense of relief he thought it would.

What did this mean in terms of Lil?

He looked at Jeremy more closely, "Who are you?"

"I'm a friend of Lil's. Well, Alethea, really. I've had a crush on that woman since high school." Jeremy's eyes widened at the audible growl Jake emitted. He quickly clarified, "Alethea, not Lil."

"You hacked into my computer for them. That was you?"

"Yes."

"Lil wanted to keep me away from my computer that day."

Jeremy nodded.

The more he thought about it, the angrier he became. It had all been a lie. The date. The fake outrage that he didn't love her. Everything. What he couldn't understand, though, was why Lil had wanted to access his files at all? Was she working for someone? He usually had a good idea of what was happening in most situations, but this one had his head

BEDDING THE BILLIONAIRE

spinning and grasping at theories. "What were you looking for?"

Jeremy wiped his greasy fingers on the hem of his checkered jacket. "I knew you were paying off programmers around the country. I know you gave them hush money, but for a rich man, you are way too cheap with your bribes. Anyway, Alethea thought Abby might be in danger. Lil said she needed proof before she'd say anything to Abby." Jeremy shrugged. "I probably shouldn't have accessed your computer, but I have a hard time saying no to Alethea. However, I got in by piggybacking on a backdoor code that I stumbled on. It was surprisingly easy so I went deeper than your email. The hacker community is not all that big. I took a guess that someone had been there before me and I was right." He smirked. "It was that West Coast weasel, Sliver. He's pathetically predictable when it comes to his attack codes and, luckily, his passwords, too. He had complete access to your mainframe. I changed his password just to piss him off. He thinks he's big-time because he's caused some crashes that have made the news." He rolled his eyes. "He's an idiot."

All this from a man who looked like he'd dressed himself in a dark closet back in the 1950s. Jake had been around long enough to understand that appearances did not equate to performance. Some of the best code writers on his team looked like they hadn't seen the light of day in years and to say that their social skills were quirky would have been kind.

Jake said, "You've just changed the outcome of the game. Trust me, you'll be well compensated for whatever infor-

205

mation you can give us."

"I don't want your money," Jeremy said.

"What do you want?"

Jeremy rubbed his chin thoughtfully. "I'm a smart guy. I may not have your level of wealth, but I've made enough selling apps and codes that I'm comfortable. There is one area that I seem to require some assistance in, however."

"Name it."

"You need to make me into a man that Alethea would want to date."

You couldn't have asked for something easier like world peace or an end to global hunger?

From what Jake had heard about Lil's friend, this guy was dreaming way out of his league. Alethea would eat him alive. She was a shark and he was a sheep, albeit very intelligent one.

Jake sought help from Victor Andrade. "Are they spiking the drinks with crazy at the party?"

Victor put a supportive hand on Jake's shoulder and said, "Son, the only one who is crazy is you if you let Lil get away. When you find a woman who is willing to risk everything for family and then for you—you marry that woman. Go tell her that you love her before it's too late."

"But I don't . . ."

The truth hit him in the stomach like a sledgehammer.

Memories of their time together flooded his mind. Lil studying at her kitchen table. Lil naked beneath him. Lil beaming with pride as she held up her daughter's artwork.

His stomach twisted painfully.

Lil at the top of the stairs, easily the most beautiful woman in the room, and yet still anxiously scanning the room as if she weren't sure she belonged. And, finally, Lil's smile when she saw him waiting for her at the bottom of the steps. He wanted to spend the rest of his life with that smile, that woman.

I do.

I do love her.

Victor tightened his hand on his shoulder. "None of this is worth a damn thing if you have no one to share it with. Go find her, Jake. When you do, don't let your pride speak for you. Pride knows nothing about love. Tell her you love her. Tell her you need her. Don't leave until she believes you."

Jake turned to leave and paused. He looked back at his parents. He wasn't even sure what he wanted to say to them, but it was difficult not to be moved by the tears he saw well in his mother's eyes. She said, "Go on, Jake. We'll be here when you get back."

He nodded.

Jeremy said, "Hey, what about me?"

Without hesitation, Jake threw his best friend under the bus. "Dominic is much better at that kind of thing than I am. Tell him that I said he owes you a favor—a huge personal favor. Then tell him what you need."

Just before exiting the door, Jake stopped and added, "You might not want to mention the part about accessing our mainframe. I'll explain it to him later."

A dead Jeremy couldn't help anyone.

Now, where would Lil go?

Chapter Fifteen

*H*OW COULD *I have been such a fool?*
Lil fought to hold back the tears that were surging within her. It wasn't like Jake had ever lied to her. He'd clearly said that he didn't love her. Why do women try to read emotion into everything a man says when really the translation was much less impressive?

"I want you," simply meant "I want to have sex with you."

"Live with me," meant "I want to have sex with you on a regular basis."

"Marry me," meant "I'm willing to share my stuff to have sex with you."

Stupid. Stupid. Stupid.

"Lil?" Her sister met her in the hallway, blocking her escape up the stairs.

Oh, great, Abby. Lil tried to stretch her trembling lips into a smile and knew she failed by the concern she saw in her sister's eyes.

Even worse, Dominic appeared behind Abby.

Lil spoke to their shoes. "I won't ruin your big night. I

just need a few minutes to freshen up."

Abby took her by the hand and simply held on until she looked up and met her eyes. "Lil, I don't care about any of this if you're not happy. What happened? I saw you and Jake earlier and you both looked like you were having a great time."

Lil sobbed her confession into one hand. "I fell in love with him, but he doesn't feel the same."

Dominic crossed his arms. "This is why he has to marry her."

Abby shook her head. "Not now, Dom."

"You like seeing your sister like this?"

"No, but you can't make people work out their issues." Abby's reasonable tone was not mirrored by her fiancé.

"Watch me."

Lil sniffed and saw the love behind the tornado. She'd misjudged Dominic. He wasn't a fantasy and he did love her sister. That his love for Abby extended to her family was humbling. Lil impatiently wiped away a tear and said, "Dominic, it will be a proud day for me when you marry my sister and I get to call you my brother."

Dominic puffed up with pride. He smiled down at his fiancé. "See, Lil agrees with me."

Abby shook her head and hugged her sister. "What are you going to do, Lil?"

Lil lifted her chin up and said, "I'm going to compose myself and then I am going to go back into the party and enjoy hearing you formally announce your engagement."

Abby pulled back a bit and looked her sister in the eye.

"And?"

Lil nodded as she made her inner resolution. "And then I'm going to return to Boston and look for a job."

Dominic said, "I own several companies in Boston. Name a job and you'll have it."

Lil smiled at her new protector, grateful for the millionth time recently that her sister had found happiness. Maybe one day she would find the same for herself. Rebellion was replaced by self-awareness. Her words were simply said and held no anger. "I don't want your charity, Dominic."

"There is no such thing as charity when it comes to family," Dominic countered.

"I don't even know what I want to do, Dom. I might take an office job for now and sign up for some art classes. I have so much I need to figure out."

"How about an entry-level position in a graphic design department? I'll tell people I don't even like you. You could sink or swim on your own," Dominic said.

"You would do that?" Lil asked, grateful that he understood.

Abby wrapped an arm around her future husband's waist and laughed up at him. "You are so full of it, Dom. I bet you couldn't go a week without calling her department head and threatening to fire him if he wasn't nice to her."

"Woman, you sorely underestimate me."

Watching the banter between the two of them removed the last of Lil's resistance. People found jobs every day by using their connections. Lil held out her hand to Dominic. "I accept your job offer."

A wide smile spread across his face as he shook her hand.

Lil added, "But I don't need your help with Jake. If we ever work it out, it will be on our terms, not yours."

Dominic started to say something and Lil cut him off. "I mean it. Promise to stay out of it."

Dominic promised nothing, but he did say, "You and Abby are so much alike."

The two sisters smiled at that.

Abby hugged her husband-to-be again. "Lil, that means that he's going to try, but he doesn't know if he can help himself."

"Do you translate everything I say because I'm not speaking English?" Dominic asked with some amusement.

"Exactly, you speak some dialect of barbarian dictator most of the time," Lil teased.

Dominic bent down and growled playfully at Abby, "Barbarian, huh? I know how much you like that."

"Okay," Lil interrupted with a laugh. "I'm heading back into the party. You two just follow when you're ready."

She walked halfway down the hallway before turning slighting to check if they were following.

They weren't.

And it didn't look like they would be for quite a while.

Lil turned away with resolve.

I want to love and be loved like that.

I want the fairy tale.

JAKE SPOTTED LIL the instant she walked through the door. He cut through diplomats and royalty with neither subtlety nor etiquette. He had to get to her side before she disappeared again.

"Lil," he said, "we need to talk."

She nodded calmly and allowed him to guide her into a room across the hall. He closed the door and his concern grew when she didn't fly at him with accusations.

She surprised him again with softly spoken words. "Jake, I am so sorry for everything I've put you through. I was looking for answers in the wrong places." He went to take her in his arms, but she moved away from him and continued. "No, I need to say this. I shouldn't have said what I did in front of your parents. I'm the last one who should judge anyone for how they deal with their family. I can't believe mine is still intact after what I've put it through. I—"

"It's okay, Lil."

"No, it's not. Words hurt and you didn't deserve my anger. You never lied—which is more than I can say about myself."

"I understand why you did it." He did. The more he'd thought about what she'd done, the more his anger had been replaced by admiration. That same fierce love that he knew she had for her daughter had driven her to protect her sister . . . and then, unbelievably, him.

He couldn't remember the last person who had risked anything for him, and Lil had risked everything. He needed to make her see that they belonged together.

"Do you? Do you really—because I'm still trying to figure out if I did it to protect Abby or because I wanted something to be wrong with her happy ending. I've wasted so much time falsely thinking we were in some sort of competition. I finally see that her happiness doesn't threaten mine. I'll find my own way. I believe that now."

Something about her tone warned him that this was goodbye and he refused to accept that possibility. "I love you, Lil."

She looked up at him from beneath her long, beautiful lashes, her amber eyes brimming with emotion. "Don't. Don't say things you don't mean."

He took her arms in his hands and held her before him. "I love you."

When he'd imagined her reaction to his declaration, he pictured her throwing her arms around him and the passion that would follow. Her steady stare was disappointing and disconcerting.

"You don't believe in love. You've said that more than once."

"I was wrong."

She studied him quietly, then shook her head. "No, you were honest and I appreciate that. You're a good man, Jake."

Then why does this still sound like goodbye?

"What do you want, Lil?" He heard the emotion in his own voice and didn't care. She couldn't leave like this.

"I'm not sure yet, but I know what I don't want. I don't want to continue our casual beginnings, I don't want to ever lie to you again, and I don't want to settle for less than everything."

"Everything?" *What more was there?* "I've told you that I'll marry you."

One tear rolled down her cheek silently. "It's not enough, Jake. I want the lover, the best friend, the hero."

"You think I can't be that?" *Hell, Dominic's fist had hurt less.*

Lil shrugged sadly and looked away. "Dominic offered me a job in Boston and I'm going to take it. It'll be a creative job and I'll take an art class or two. I have to find my footing."

"So, that's it?" He strove for calm. "You want to end this?"

"I don't know."

"I do." He kissed her with everything he was feeling. He kissed her until she was shaking with passion against him. "Stay," he whispered. "We'll figure the rest out."

She pulled away. "No. It would be too easy to let passion decide this." She backed another step away from him and opened the door to the hallway. "Please leave me alone for now, Jake. I need time to figure this out. You do, too."

He went to the door and watched her disappear back into the party.

A disheartened male voice broke the silence that followed. "Man, if you can't get the girl, I'm screwed."

Jeremy stood beside Jake, watching Lil disappear into the crowd. "I'm going to marry her."

The poorly-suited man gave Jake a sympathetic pat on the back. "Of course you are, man. Of course you are."

Chapter Sixteen

JAKE SPENT THE next couple of days introducing Jeremy to how Corisi Enterprises looked from the right side of the computer. In addition to the image consultant Dominic had found for Jeremy, Jake had offered him an office in their main building. At first he'd balked at the idea of formally joining a team, but the lure of working, even temporarily, with the Waltons proved too tempting for him to pass on in the end.

If the initial tests were correct, the Chinese server was patched and ready to go. No more surprise rewriting of the codes. No more unauthorized access to emails or mainframes. Between his parents and Jeremy, Jake doubted there was another company on the planet as secure as Corisi Enterprises had become.

This should have been a time to celebrate, but Jake found no real joy in the news. He lingered in the Corisi Towers long past when everyone had left for the day. He didn't want to admit it to himself, but he didn't want to go home.

Dominic walked in Jake's office, plopped in one of the

chairs in front of his desk, and propped his feet up on it. "Stop sulking."

Jake leaned forward and pushed his friend's feet off his desk. "I'm not sulking."

Unperturbed, Dominic stretched his legs and crossed his ankles on the floor before him. "Do you know what your problem is?"

"I'm sure you're going to tell me."

Dominic smiled. "You're over-thinking this. Normally I respect that side of you, but it doesn't work with women."

"Spare me the Cro-Magnon tips on romance."

"I don't care what your IQ is—you're an idiot if you think that sitting in this office is going to get her back."

"She said she needed time to figure out a few things."

"That is code for, '*Get off your ass and show me that you care.*'"

"How have you never had a restraining order taken out against you?"

"Say what you will, but my woman is planning a wedding and yours is . . ." Dominic snapped his fingers as if he'd just remembered something. "Oh, yes, you don't know what she's doing because you're giving her time to figure things out."

Jake pushed his chair back and stood. "What's scary is that you're beginning to make sense to me." He needed to take action now before she figured him right out of her life.

Dominic joined his friend near the door and gave him an encouraging slap on the back. "The trick is selective hearing. Women tell you what they want; they just throw in all that other shit to confuse you. Now stop thinking and go get her."

"You're right," Jake said and suddenly he knew exactly how to do it.

A WEEK LATER, Lil was eating a salad at a small table in a café of a downtown office building. True to his word, Dominic had found her a job immediately upon her return. Mrs. Duhamel had flown back to Boston with her, determined to watch Colby until they found a nanny both she and Lil could agree on. Although it was difficult to leave Colby, there was something invigorating about the challenge of learning a new job. She didn't know much about graphic design, but not surprisingly, the position offered as much on the job training as she wanted.

Okay, there were definitely perks to being Dominic's *little sister.*

A shadow fell across the table. Lil looked up and her breath caught in her throat.

Jake.

"Please forgive my boldness, but when I saw you I had to come over and introduce myself. Jake Walton." He held out a hand in greeting.

She shook it, her eyes narrowing suspiciously.

What was he playing at?

"Lillian Dartley."

He put a hand on the back of the chair across from her. "Is this seat taken?"

"What if I said yes?"

RUTH CARDELLO

He didn't smile. "I would come back every day until you said it wasn't."

She gulped. Her voice was a bit of a croak as she said, "Please. Sit."

He sat and leaned back in the chair. "So, you work here?"

"Yes." Then, because she didn't know what else to say, she said, "This is my second week."

"You like it?"

"It's okay." *Getting more interesting by the minute.* "Everyone is very nice."

"I miss you." He reached across the table and took her hand lightly. "You and Colby."

Lil's hand shook in his. "What is this, Jake? What are you doing here?"

He turned her hand over in his and curled his fingers through hers. "You were right. We have things we need to figure out, but we shouldn't do it alone. I want to hear about your first week at work, to see the paintings you bring home from your art class. I want to be there when Colby takes her first step. I'm not going to settle for less than everything."

Tears welled in Lil's eyes. She wanted so badly to believe, but she couldn't.

He asked, "Do you think your boss would let you take an extended lunch?"

"I think he'd be fired if he didn't," Lil said with a rueful smile. Working for Dominic's company wasn't exactly like getting a job on her own merit. There was a price to pay for being associated with such a powerful man, but Lil was becoming more comfortable with it each day. Life could be much worse. Curiosity got the best of her. "Why?"

"I have a surprise for you."

Instead of heading out the front door, Jake led her to the elevator and pressed the button for the roof. There in the middle of the landing pad was a luxury helicopter with a huge red ribbon on the side of it. Lil had seen helicopters before, but none like this. It was longer than most and had two distinct sections, a front area for the pilot and a passenger area that looked as comfortable and private as a limousine. Lil cupped her eyes and peeked into one of the round windows. Jake opened the door to the passenger compartment and said, "You can look closer than that, it's yours."

Lil looked at the six ivory, leather seats that flanked a lushly-carpeted, center aisle and turned back to Jake. "You got me a helicopter?"

Jake shrugged. "I heard you hate flowers. The interior is completely soundproof so you don't have to worry about headphones for Colby."

"This is crazy."

"No, this is how we start over." He handed her a card. "Call this number and a pilot will be here in about thirty minutes. Boston to New York takes about an hour and a half, but you'll never fight traffic. Colby's car seat will clip right in."

"So you want me to come down to New York more often?"

"If you want to. Or I'll come up here. I know how to be

your lover. I'm working on the rest of your list."

Best friend?

Hero?

He's serious.

Oh, God, he's serious.

"I have one other surprise," he said.

Lil wasn't sure she could take another one, her heart was already beating double-time in her chest. "I've hired a real estate agent and he compiled a list of lofts available in both Boston and New York."

A loft? Had Jake decided that instead of marrying her he would stash her somewhere convenient? "I don't think—"

Jake pulled her against him and tipped her chin up so she was looking at him. "Let me do this for you. I know you want to do everything yourself, but it will just be a large empty space. You're the one who will have to hone your craft and fill it with artwork."

"What are you saying?" Then she understood and gasped, afraid to believe she had heard him correctly. "You're looking for an art studio for me?"

"If you want one."

"If I want one?" She laughed and cried at the same time. Somehow this man saw past what she said and knew her heart. She wasn't walking away this time. "Okay."

"Okay, you'll accept the helicopter? Okay, you'll let me buy you a studio?"

"Okay, I'll marry you," she said simply.

He swayed a bit on his feet then crushed her to him.

She added, "I do love the helicopter, but what really got

me was . . ."

"My charm?" he asked with a tint of humor.

She shook her head with a smile. "Not quite."

He gave her a playful squeeze. "My persistence?"

She laughed up at him. "It took you long enough to show up here."

He smiled back at her, knowing that she would eventually tell him what he was waiting to hear.

Lil looked him in the eye and said, "What got me was how well you know me. Not the me I pretend to be or the one I was convinced I had to be—just me. Somehow you sorted through all the crap I said and heard what I needed."

Jake shook his head and said, "I hate when Dominic is right."

That piqued Lil's curiosity. "About what?"

Jake leaned down and kissed her until she forgot what they were discussing.

Until her only thought was that dreams really do come true.

When he finally rested his forehead on hers and their ragged breathing began to calm, he said, "I know you're looking for a hero, Lil, but you've already earned that title. Our server is clean and ready to go online, issue free."

Even though the topic meant downshifting a bit emotionally, Lil knew it needed to be discussed before they could move forward. "I'm so glad. Jeremy had the solution?"

"He had a large piece of the puzzle. My parents worked the rest out. However, his insight was invaluable as far as debugging the system in time to meet our deadline."

Lil absently played with the hair just behind one of his ears. "Speaking of your parents—are they staying for the wedding?"

"I have no idea. For now, they are staying with the Andrades. It's going to take us a while to put the past behind us, but they seem to sincerely want to be part of my life."

"You should have Dominic invite them, Jake. They're family."

He smiled down at her. "Is this what I'm signing on for—a lifetime of you telling me what to do?"

"Absolutely," she said without missing a beat.

He sobered suddenly and said, "I love you, Lil."

She kissed his lips softly. "And I love you, Jake."

"Do you want to go back to work now?"

Lil rubbed herself playfully against him. "Surprisingly, not as much as I thought I would."

Within moments she was grateful that Jake had invested in a large and remarkably private helicopter interior. He whipped open the door and laid her across the off-white carpeted flooring.

With precision, he undressed himself and then her. Then his hands slowed as they explored her, worshipped her, guided her to a place where coherent thought was no longer possible. Although the passion remained strong between them, this time there was no need to rush. Knowing that they had the rest of their lives added a depth to their lovemaking. Each touch meant more. Each kiss lingered longer so they could savor it.

He paused to put on a condom and whispered against her lips, "I want to do this right. First marriage and then a houseful of kids."

She laughed against his lips. "Don't you mean first marriage, then sex, then kids . . ."

"Oh, no, I never agreed with that order," he said and claimed her mouth with his.

She lost herself in his touch, his kiss, the feel of him teasing her wetness and said, "I could be persuaded to your way of thinking."

"I'll do my best," he said, and his best did not disappoint.

Completely spent, she collapsed onto his chest. He rolled onto his side and tucked her head onto his strong bicep. "Convinced?"

She winked at him and said, "I'm not sure yet. We might have to do that again."

He growled down at her and said, "Really?"

"The whole thing or just that last part? Whatever."

He ran a teasing finger from her jaw, lightly across the swell of her breasts and down the curve of one of her hips. "I've always loved helicopters, but now I have an even deeper appreciation for them."

Lil reached down, wrapped her hand softly around the part of him that was already coming back to life and asked, "Is your private jet this comfortable?"

He hardened in her hand. "I'll have new carpeting put in all of my vehicles."

A good idea, but one that would have to wait.

For now, the helicopter provided just enough privacy for Lil to confidently trail kisses down Jake's flat abdomen and lower.

Chapter Seventeen

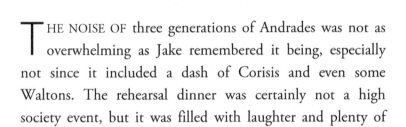

T HE NOISE OF three generations of Andrades was not as overwhelming as Jake remembered it being, especially not since it included a dash of Corisis and even some Waltons. The rehearsal dinner was certainly not a high society event, but it was filled with laughter and plenty of children.

Colby bounced happily on Jake's knee while the main course was being served. Other families might have sent the children to another room to eat, but the Andrades merely extended their table and their hearts to include all in what could only be described as a feast.

Lil was seated next to him, happily chatting about babies with one of Stephan's cousins.

Victor Andrade stood at the head of the table and the room fell silent. "It is my great pleasure to open my home—well, the Andrade home—" His brother raised a glass of wine to him with a tolerant smile. ". . . to our new family. Some people become family through blood. Some people through marriage. Others find their way into your life and your heart through friendship. Raise a glass to all of our family tonight . . . those who share our name and those who we have come to care deeply for. There is no greater fortune than to be surrounded by so much love. Dominic and Abby, may your life and your table always be as full as it is tonight."

Dominic raised his glass and drank to the toast. Everyone followed suit. Abby used her napkin to wipe away tears that were running freely down her cheeks.

Jake looked to his left and saw his parents watching him quietly. He lifted the child on his lap and held her out toward his father. "Dad, do you want to hold her?"

His father took her into his arms as if she were the most fragile of creatures. "So, this will be our first grandchild?"

Jake's heart swelled. "Yes. Lil had the biological father sign off his rights before she was born. I'm going to adopt her the same day I marry Lil."

His mother took her from her husband and hugged her. "Jim, it looks like we're going to have to start believing in Santa Claus."

His father turned and looked at his son and said, "We will, Jake. This time we will. I could even write an algorithm to prove how he could make it around the world in one night."

Colby reached out and pulled on her future grandfather's nose. He laughed, "This one is going to be trouble, Jake."

Jake smiled and glanced at Lil. "Just like her mom."

Lil turned around when she heard Jake's voice. "What are you talking about?"

Jake put his arm around Lil and said, "How every life needs a little chaos."

"Wait, I'm the chaos? You'll pay for that!"

He laughed. He didn't mind the way she doled out punishment.

In fact, he rather liked it.

His father asked, "Jake, whatever happened to Jeremy? We haven't seen him in days."

"It seems that his makeover is going to take longer than we thought. The consultant we hired thought it would go faster if he was on site for a while."

Lil laughed. "Sounds serious. He's that determined to get Alethea?"

Jake nodded solemnly. "Men will do all sorts of crazy things for women. He did give me a gift, though, before he left."

Lil cocked her head to the side.

Jake took out his phone and said, "He hacked into a certain news station's files and made a ringtone for me. Now whenever you call me, I hear this."

Lil's voice played clearly from his phone when he pressed a button. "Of course I find Jake Walton sexy, who wouldn't?"

Lil slapped his shoulder. "Out of that whole interview, that's all you heard, wasn't it?"

Jake nodded with a huge smile on his face.

He played it again and held the phone out of her reach when she grabbed for it. "It's all that mattered."

Chapter Eighteen

L IL MET HER sister's eyes in the mirror and dabbed a happy tear away before it could smudge her makeup.

"Are you sure the veil is on securely?" Abby asked.

"I can have the stylist check it again, but I think short of stapling it on, it's as secure as it gets."

Abby turned and Lil was once again moved by the glow on her sister's face. The paparazzi would love her—not that they would have a chance to snap a single photo. With the Andrade's blessing, the couple had flown less than a hundred guests to Isola Santos for a highly private wedding. Immense air-conditioned tents covered the lawn and led to a discrete area that would allow the couple to marry with the ocean as a backdrop to their ceremony. There was only one photographer and he'd signed a non-disclosure contract.

Although Alethea was not attending the wedding, she'd sent a wedding present—a schematic breakdown of the weaknesses she'd found both at Dominic's engagement party and in his plans for the island wedding. Abby hadn't warmed up to her enough to invite her to the wedding, but she was beginning to soften her stance against her. After all, Alethea had played a role in saving Corisi Enterprises.

The only one who wasn't presently happy with Lil's best friend was Dominic's head of security. Rumor had it that he was furious when he read her report, especially since she'd noted that he was "easily distracted" from his duties. That was Al, making friends wherever she went.

My sister is getting married today.

Today.

Three weeks hadn't been much time to prepare for a wedding, but since the budget had been so generous—it had come together seamlessly. Amazing what people could accomplish when they worked on commission and the bride could have whatever she wanted.

Concepts for wedding dresses had arrived almost immediately from several well-known designers and it was no surprise that Abby had chosen something simple: a white strapless, silk gown with layers of lace that covered both the dress and Abby's arms and shoulders in the classic style of Grace Kelly. Her bouquet was a nosegay of white wild orchids, white peonies and mini calla lilies. Abby's most stunning accessory was the huge smile that hadn't dimmed since she'd met Lil for breakfast that morning.

Lil looked down her own iridescent, charcoal chiffon dress. The body of it was shirred and fitted from the strapless, ruffled bodice to the mid-thigh hemline that boasted a detachable flowing skirt. Mrs. Duhamel had found the perfect compromise-dress, floor-length to satisfy Abby and sizzling and short in one easy step for Lil. Nicole and Maddy had been easy to talk into wearing the spicy bridesmaid's dress, but Zhang had been an altogether different matter. She had also been the wildcard in the wedding party. Maddy's husband, Richard, and Nicole's fiancé, Stephan, were natural choices for groomsmen. Maddy convinced Abby that choosing a groomsman for Zhang had to be done as carefully as if they were matchmaking.

Lil smiled at the memory of how they had finally chosen a fourth groomsman.

Dominic had declined on having a bachelor party, saying that he'd had quite enough wild days in his past. In the spirit of that decision, in lieu of a bachelorette party the women had gathered at one of Dominic's homes with a few bottles of champagne for a high-tech slide show of men Dominic knew well enough to ask to be part of his wedding party.

Maddy had suggested that, to keep it fun, the candidates must either be royalty or be on *Forbes* list of most influential men. The selection process was as much fun as any night on the town would have been. Maddy cued up the photos on a large screen in the home's private movie theater. Nicole read a detailed description of each man. Pros and cons were discussed and then Maddy used her photoshopping skills to superimpose Zhang and the potential escort into the same photo walking down an aisle, arm in arm.

Even if the candidates were wildly inappropriate, some were kept in the proposal packet simply for the humor of it. Too tall. Too short. Too old. Too young. Too greasy. Too uptight. Too much facial hair. Too bald.

At first Zhang had stoically held to her stand that she had no preference.

Lil poured her a glass of champagne.

"No, thank you," Zhang politely refused the beverage.

"Everyone drinks at weddings," Lil insisted.

Zhang motioned with her hand at the movie theater around them and said, "This is not even the wedding."

"True," Lil laughed and pushed the drink into Zhang's hand. "But you're going to spend a significant amount of time with whoever we pick. There is the rehearsal, the wedding itself, photos, maybe even some dancing. You don't think you care now, but do you really want to spend the wedding holding onto *this* Prince Charming?"

Lil motioned to Maddy who brought up a photo of a man they had actually found on a world's scariest criminals website, but Zhang didn't need to know that. Lil said, "Sober, you don't seem able to decide. We can choose for you if you want, but *this* is what might happen." Maddy cued up the photo of Zhang and a long haired, mostly toothless criminal walking down an aisle together.

Shamelessly, Lil added a final zinger. "Maddy even has the software that could show you what your children would look like if ended up with him." The photo Maddy produced was as hilarious as it was hideous.

Zhang downed the glass of champagne in one gulp and replaced the glass.

Abby looked on, shaking her head. "Lil, you are . . ."

Maddy answered for her, "My hero!"

Abby smiled sympathetically at Zhang and said, "You know, I can call her off. At least, I can try."

Zhang took the second glass of champagne Lil offered

her and smiled in resignation. She and Lil were polar opposites, but somehow they had connected and were building a friendship through the planning of the wedding together. She joked, "I had no idea that the American custom was to choose a groomsman worthy of bearing children with or I would have paid more attention to the previous ones. Please, cue up the next one."

Nicole read the corresponding card. "Sheikh Rachid bin Amir al Hantan, Crown Prince of Najriad—a small country but gaining prominence for their technology as well as their oil."

Lil shot a quick look at Zhang and saw her interest before she was able to conceal it again. *Thank you champagne.* Lil prompted, "He's hot."

Abby added, "I think Dominic actually knows him pretty well. He either graduated from Harvard the year before or the year after Dom and Jake did. I've heard him mention him before." She smiled. "I agree—he's hot." Everyone looked at her. "What, I'm getting married, but I'm not blind. That man is gorgeous."

Zhang said, "He wouldn't be our worst choice."

Lil said, "Cue up how they would look as a couple."

Maddy clapped. "Oh, we have to pick him. He's perfect for you."

Nicole warned, "Just remember, gorgeous men have big . . ." She paused for dramatic emphasis. "Egos," she finished with a laugh.

Everyone laughed—even Zhang.

Abby said, "If he got out of line, I'm sure Zhang could

put him firmly back in his place."

Zhang straightened a little defensively and said, "Sometimes I'm shy around men." A round of laughter swept the room, but Zhang didn't join in. She added, "You don't work as much as I do and date much."

Maddy said, "Oh, my God that is so cute." When Zhang shot her a glare, she back-peddled nervously. "I mean cute in the least condescending way I could have said it. It's just that I can picture you staring into those beautiful dark eyes—temporarily at a loss for what to say—waiting for him to kiss you for the first time."

Lil said, "You've been reading too many of those romances again."

Maddy countered, "Hello, I married a French man. I live romance. And who do you think suggested that Jake be the one to move you into a new place? Hmm?"

Lil threw some popcorn at the tiny woman's head. "That was you?"

Maddy laughed and removed a piece of popcorn from her hair. "You can thank me whenever you're ready. Matchmaking is my gift."

Zhang said, "I'm not looking for a man."

Maddy nodded her approval. "That's always the best time to find one. I vote for the sheikh. All in favor say 'aye.'"

Everyone except Zhang chimed in their approval.

Maddy played around with her laptop until a photo of a beautiful baby, somewhat distorted, appeared on the screen. "Come on, look at how cute your children would be."

Zhang stiffened. "I don't care which man we choose

today."

Lil leaned closer to her and said softly, "Really, then why are you blushing?"

Before World War III broke out, Abby quickly interceded. "I'll have Dominic call him."

Lil said, "Should we pick a runner-up in case he says no?"

Everyone looked at her like she'd asked if they should have a plan in case the world stopped turning on the wedding day. Dominic got what Dominic wanted—that hadn't changed regardless of how much Abby had tamed him. Lil laughed, "You're right. Meet your date to the wedding, Zhang—Prince I-should-be-an-underwear-model Rachid."

Zhang laughed and shook her head.

Lil said, "See, if you get shy just imagine him in a clothing catalogue. That always cracks me up."

"Lil, are you listening?" Abby said in a tone that implied she'd asked it before and gotten no response.

Her voice brought Lil back to the present.

Lil said, "I was just thinking about Zhang and her prince. What a shame he couldn't make the rehearsal. I hope he's not a total stick in the mud."

Abby spun in the mirror and adjusted the back of her dress again. "He had some business he couldn't get out of. Dominic said it was important enough that he understood. Some border dispute that his country is having with one of their neighbors. Whatever it was, it looks like it has temporarily been quelled because he's here today."

"I'm glad. I'd really like to see Zhang have a good time," Lil said and fixed Abby's train for the fiftieth time.

Abby cautioned, "Lil, don't push her. Whatever happens—happens."

"I know. It's just that she's all tough and reserved on the surface, but I think she's really sad on the inside. She told me the story about her parents. Do you know that although she was born into a very poor family and it would have been easier for them if she'd been a boy, her father celebrated her? She said he always told her that she could do anything a man could do. She certainly proved him right, but it's almost like she thinks she can't be successful and be a woman. The fact that she's wearing a dress for your wedding is a testament to how much she cares about you. I don't get why it's such a big deal to her. Does she think she'll lose it all if she wears a dress one time?"

"I told you, no one is immune to fear."

Something in her sister's voice gave her pause. "Are you nervous about today, Abby?" She didn't look nervous, but the closer she and her sister became the more Lil saw that Abby worried just as much as she did—she just hid it better.

Abby gave her a shaky smile. "I love him, Lil, but sometimes I wonder if I can do this. Did you see his side of the invitation list? What if I make a fool out of myself out there today? I have to study before I meet new people so I'll know how to address them; actually study with Marie. Is that really the woman Dominic wants at his side for the rest of his life?"

Lil hugged her sister. "Dominic told me that he's a better man because of you. I don't think he gives a flying squirrel if you mess up when you greet some head of state. And didn't you tell me that beneath all the money, these people are just as messed up as we are?"

Abby sniffed and straightened. "I did."

How had she never seen that Abby needed her as much as she needed Abby? "Then just be yourself, because that's who Dominic fell for and who he wants to grow old with. If you stay true to yourself and true to him, everything else will work out."

Abby smiled. "When did you become so wise?"

"It's a natural byproduct of being raised by two incredible women. You and Mom taught me everything I know about love."

"Don't you dare make me cry and ruin my mascara!"

"So I can't say it?"

"I'm warning you, Lil!" Abby said with a half-laugh, half-cry.

"We'll stop by and have your makeup retouched on our way to meet up with the girls. Don't worry." She picked up the short train of her sister's gown and said, "Lead the way, Soon-to-be-Mrs. Corisi."

Abby took a fortifying deep breath and started walking.

From behind her, Lil said softly, "Always better together, Abby."

Abby turned, wiping a tear from her cheek, but smiling. "You're awful."

"No," Lil answered simply, "just finally grateful."

WITH GROWING AMUSEMENT, Jake watched his friend

impatiently pace the room. "Are you sure you don't want a drink?"

"Is everyone here now?" Dominic asked.

"Yes, they are all just down the hallway."

"Why the hell aren't they in here? I thought you said we had to run through some last-minute change Abby had made to the ceremony."

"Amazingly enough, I'm the only one, outside of your lovely bride to be, who can stand you when you're like this."

Dominic boomed, "Like what?"

Jake just looked at him until Dominic ran a frustrated hand through his hair. "I don't like the waiting part."

"Really? I never would have guessed."

There was a knock on the door.

Mrs. Duhamel poked her head in. "Everyone dressed?"

Jake said, "Yes, Marie."

She walked up to Dominic, straightened the front of his tuxedo and reached up to put a wayward lock of hair back into place. "How are you boys holding up?"

Jake laughed, "He's a wreck."

Dominic growled but didn't deny it.

Marie made a tsk sound at Jake and said, "It's not nice to tease him, Jake. Wait until it's your turn with Lil. You'll be just as bad."

"Is everything set for us to fly out tonight?"

"Yes, the jet is packed and all you have to do is get on and go."

"And on the other side?"

"I've lined up two Realtors who know South America

well. You should have some viable sites chosen by the end of the week."

"And Abby still thinks we're going to Spain?" Dominic asked.

Marie nodded. "You'll have to call me and tell me what she says when she hears that instead of staying in a castle on her honeymoon, she's going to spend a week in a variety of South American countries buying land for the schools you're going to build there."

"I hope she loves it."

"She will," Marie said and then snapped her fingers as a thought came to her. "Before I forget, Rosella and Thomas are in the room across from the groomsmen. Nicole and Stephan went in to see them for a short visit. You should go see them, too, before you go down the aisle. Rosella won't come here because she doesn't want to intrude, but she's your mother and she should be part of this."

Dominic took the older woman into what looked like a bone crushing hug. "Then I am an incredibly lucky man because I have two mothers now."

Jake mocked his friend's display of emotion. "Marie, can you believe what Abby has done to my friend?"

Marie turned back to Jake and said, "True love makes people stronger not weaker, Jake. Remember that. I still miss my husband every day, but I can go on because something as strong as we had makes me believe in an afterlife. Treasure these times, boys. Love your women with all you have because the day will come when you must part from them—however temporarily. Arguments will happen but always apologize—even when you're not sure that you're the one who was wrong. Pride is a cold bed partner."

Jake looked across at Dominic. "I hope she's not about to explain the birds and bees to us."

Marie folded her arms in disapproval. "You boys know a bit too much about that already if you asked me."

Jake put an arm around the woman he'd grown to think of like family. "How else are we going to make those little babies you love so much?"

That got a smile from Marie. "You'd better marry Lil soon if that is your intention."

"Oh, I intend to, Marie. I intend to." He pocketed Dominic and Abby's wedding rings and said, "Come on, Dom. Let's go see Rosella while we still have time. Your afterlife will come sooner than you think if we're late to the altar."

JUST OUTSIDE A large white tent where everyone was seated facing a small altar and the ocean, Lil stood beside Zhang. "So, did you meet the sheikh yet?"

Zhang's mask of composure was firmly in place. "Not yet, but I'm sure everything will go smoothly."

"I asked Jake to look into something for me. Do you know that Prince Rachid is completely unattached at the moment? I guess his father had chosen someone for him, but he refused. He didn't want to marry a pampered princess. Maybe he likes his woman with a bit more backbone." Lil wiggled her eyebrows at her friend.

Zhang picked up her bouquet and rolled her eyes. "I can

assure you that I'm not interested."

Lil reached out and lightly touched the forearm of the beautifully proud woman before her. "There is no press here today. No one to record an impulsive action if you decide to take one."

Zhang didn't soften, but nor did she pull away.

"For just one day, don't be Zhang the billionaire. Don't be the woman you think you have to be. You are stunning in that dress. Make that sheikh squirm."

Zhang sighed. "I wouldn't even know how."

Lil smiled. "Yes, you do. You just have to let go and nature will take its course." Lil made a quick grab for Zhang's clutch and opened it, removing her phone. "Step one, no texting. No phone calls. You are not a business woman today. You're simply a gorgeous woman in a beautiful dress."

Amazingly enough, Zhang didn't protest—reaffirming Lil's belief that this was something her friend yearned to do.

"Step two," Lil continued, "you pinkie swear to me that you will kiss that sheikh before midnight tonight."

"Pinkie swear?"

Lil curled her pinkie finger around Zhang's. "It's the most solemn vow."

Zhang smiled. "Americans are so strange."

"Don't try to get off the hook. Swear it. I dare you to."

Zhang's smile widened. "I'm not afraid of your little game."

"Really? Prove it."

Zhang curled her pinkie around Lil's. "I pinkie swear it."

Lil laughed and released her.

Zhang shook her head, but laughed with her. "You are trouble, Lil Dartley."

Shamelessly, Lil shrugged. "It's who I am."

"And the world is better for it, my friend."

The roving wedding planner intruded into their conversation. "Are we ready to line up?"

The two women nodded and moved into their places behind Abby.

The music started and Abby turned around before starting her walk. "I'm so glad you're here, Lil."

Holding her bouquet in one hand, Lil gave her sister a little nudge with her other and said, "Get going unless you want me to make you cry again."

Abby gave her a teary smile.

Too late.

DOMINIC STOOD TALL and proud at his spot before the altar, waiting for his soon-to-be-bride to join him. The four men who flanked one side of him were an equally impressive sight and one that not many women in the audience, married or not, would soon forget. The female minister they had chosen as their officiant looked on with quiet grace.

When Abby reached Dominic, he took both of her hands in his and they turned to face each other in front of the altar. Lil and the bridesmaids took their places on the bride's side of the altar and the minister began to speak. As Lil listened to the officiant, she couldn't help but look across at Jake and think that they would be making vows to each other one day soon. He winked at her as if he had heard her thoughts and had been thinking something quite similar.

"Dearest friends and family, we are gathered here today to witness and celebrate the union of Dominic Corisi and Abigail Dartley in marriage. When they approached me about performing their ceremony, I wasn't sure if I was qualified since my experience has been limited to small weddings in my local chapel. However, after two minutes with them, I saw that they were no different than any other couple I have married. They are deeply devoted to each other, passionately in love, and committed to making the world a better place through the strength of their love. They have written their own vows for today. Do you have the rings?"

Jake handed the rings to Dominic and said something that made the couple smile.

Dominic cleared his throat and said, "Abigail Dartley, today I take you as my wife. From this day on, I promise to be faithful and honest, loving and supportive. I promise to listen to your wise counsel and confess when I decide to disregard it."

Lil bit her lip to stop the laugh that his comment inspired. Her family was never going to be the same. Yes, it was going to be much, much better.

Dominic continued, "I promise to forgive more, destroy less, and to savor every day with you. I give you this ring as a symbol that everything I am and everything I have will be yours now and forever." He placed a wedding band on Abby's finger.

Abby held out his wedding band, took his hand in hers and said, "Dominic Corisi, today I take you as my husband. I promise to be faithful and honest, loving and supportive. I promise to adore you as you are and gracefully accept your apologies each time you discover that I was right. I promise to risk more, judge less and to savor every day with you. I give you this ring as a symbol that everything I am and everything I have will be yours now and forever." She placed the gold band on Dominic's finger.

The officiant said, "By exchanging rings and vows today, Dominic and Abby you have sworn your life and your allegiance to each other. Time and tragedy will test this bond. When it does, remember the love you felt this day and stay true to your commitment. Dominic and Abigail, I now pronounce you husband and wife. You may kiss the bride."

The crowd held their breath as a man who had once been known only for what he had accumulated and threatened gently kissed the lips of his new wife and hugged her to him with such love that it was impossible to look away.

Everyone stood and the officiant said, "It is a great honor for me to introduce, for the first time, Mr. and Mrs. Dominic Corisi."

Lil looked across to Jake and knew that he, like her, had been imagining their wedding, their vows . . . their first kiss as a married couple. To music and applause, Lil linked arms with Jake and followed Dominic and Abby down the aisle and out of the tent to meet the photographer. They would have their day, but the next hour or so was all about filling Dominic and Abby's wedding album.

AFTER ENTERING THE reception with Jake and the rest of the bridal party, Lil turned to him and said, "I want to run in and check on Colby really quickly before everything gets started. I love the nanny we chose, but I—"

Jake pulled her against him and whispered into her ear, "I'll go with you."

Lil laughed and pulled out of his grasp. "No way. I'm not missing the toast because we get distracted out there."

"I love the way you distract me," he growled and reached for her again.

She edged away. "That's the problem. I am not going to mess this up. If you don't come with me I can be back here in ten minutes."

"I could control myself," he claimed.

She leaned in and snuck a quick kiss while he was defending his honor then slid back out of his reach. "But could I?" she teased softly.

His face flushed slightly with excitement. "I think I could make ten minutes work."

"That's nothing to brag about," Lil joked and loved how he opened his mouth, but didn't have a witty comeback. It meant that she had indeed succeeded in shaking him up. She snuck in for one more quick kiss and said, "I'll be right back."

His mouth curled in amusement. "I'll be here, plotting my revenge."

She knew it was the kind of payback she would likely enjoy, so she felt safe enough to tease him more. "If you're that sensitive, you've picked the wrong woman."

This time he did grab her and held her against his growing excitement. "I wouldn't change a thing about you, Lil, but that doesn't mean I won't prove to you later exactly how much I can accomplish in ten minutes."

He leaned down to kiss her and she couldn't think of a single witty response. He kissed her until she forgot what had been so funny and desperately wanted to beg him to leave with her.

When he raised his head she touched a trembling hand to his lips and stared at the elegant, emerald-cut diamond on her left hand. Was this really her life? Could something this wonderful really happen to her?

He sensed her change of mood and tried to lighten it by saying, "Would it help if I promised at least twenty minutes?"

She smacked his chest lightly. In the safety of his arms, she admitted her fear. "Sometimes I still don't believe this is real. I mean, Abby deserves a happy ending, but I've done everything wrong. I shouldn't be this happy."

Jake pulled her closer and kissed her on the forehead. Then he bent and let his words tickle her left ear. "If love was only for the perfect, what a sad and lonely world it would it be. We are the culmination of every good and bad choice we've ever made. Your mistakes have made you into an incredibly fierce and loving woman; one I am head over heels in love with. They have filled your life with friends who are willing to risk jail for you. They brought Colby into the world. One of your mistakes even saved our company. So, don't change, Lil. You keep making those mistakes and you just might save us all."

The next kiss they shared had less to do with raw passion and more to do with two hearts reaching out to each other and promising each other forever.

The wedding planner broke into their intimate moment and said, "Are you both ready to say your toasts?"

Lil smiled at Jake and nodded. "I guess I'll check Colby after we do that." She winked at her man. "We'll go together."

He groaned, "Are you trying to make me forget my speech?"

She laughed wickedly and whispered a hot suggestion into his ear.

Game on.

FROM A LARGE stone patio, tucked beneath one of Jake's arms, Lil waved again at the private jet that was now only lights disappearing into the night sky. "She's going to love Spain."

Jake said, "Even more than you know."

Lil looked up at him suspiciously, "What does that mean?"

He smiled. "I'll let her tell you."

"Oh, no, we don't do any more secrets."

His smile turned wicked. "You might be able to persuade me to tell you."

"You are insatiable, do you know that?"

He looked rather proud of himself. "Is that a complaint?"

Lil thought about how much she'd enjoyed the reason

they had missed the dinner portion of the wedding and reluctantly returned just in time to see the cutting of the cake. "No, but now I won't be able to use that elevator without blushing."

"Especially if the security system has a camera in there."

"Oh, my God! I'm never going to be able to look the security people in the eye again."

Jake laughed. "I'll talk to them and if there is a camera I'll have the video erased. Well, maybe copied and then erased."

"Just erased!" Lil elbowed him lightly.

Jake merely smiled.

Security cameras. She should have thought about that when she told Zhang to wander on the wild side.

Stretching his neck a bit to see more of the runway, Jake said, "I don't see Rachid's plane anymore. It's not like him to leave without saying goodbye. When I talked to him earlier he said he had something he wanted to ask me. That's interesting."

Lil shrugged. "The last time I saw him he was dancing, if you could call that dancing, with Zhang. They looked like they were really hitting it off."

Jake scratched his cheek thoughtfully. "Have you seen Zhang since then?"

Lil checked the contents of the clutch she'd carried with her through the entire evening. "No, but I still have her phone. You don't think . . ."

Jake cocked his head to the side as if considering the idea, then shook his head. "No, that's not Zhang. If her phone and her plane are here, she's here somewhere. She'd never leave without them." He shook his head again. "No. Not Zhang."

Lil turned Zhang's phone in her hand and considered the possibilities. With a grin, she turned it off and placed it back within her purse. *Good for you, Zhang. I did pick the right dress.*

Jake returned his attention to a much more intimate topic. He wiggled his eyebrows, likely remembering her earlier promise of how they would end their evening as he asked, "Ready?"

His sexy question implied tonight, but she pondered past that.

Am I ready for all of this? This man? This life change? Everything this means for me and for my child?

Jake entwined his fingers with hers and the answer came to her—strong and absolute.

I am.

I'm finally ready.

"Yes," she said and meant it with every fiber of her being.

Hand in hand, they walked into the rest of their lives together.

THE END

Don't miss a release or a sale.
Sign up for my newsletter today.
forms.aweber.com/form/58/1378607658.htm

About the Author

Ruth Cardello was born the youngest of 11 children in a small city in southern Massachusetts. She spent her young adult years moving as far away as she could from her large extended family. She lived in Boston, Paris, Orlando, New York—then came full circle and moved back to New England. She now happily lives one town over from the one she was born in. For her, family trumped the warmer weather and international scene.

She was an educator for 20 years, the last 11 as a kindergarten teacher. When her school district began cutting jobs, Ruth turned a serious eye toward her second love– writing and has never been happier. When she's not writing, you can find her chasing her children around her small farm, riding her horses, or connecting with her readers online.

Contact Ruth:

Website: RuthCardello.com
Email: Ruthcardello@gmail.com
FaceBook: Author Ruth Cardello
Twitter: @RuthieCardello

Made in the USA
Middletown, DE
28 November 2022

16223613R00146